Crashing Together

Amelia Judd

Cover design by LLewellen Designs
Edited by Karen Dale Harris
Proofread by Daisycakes Creative Services

Published by Mitchell Davis Press, LLC

www.ameliajudd.com

ISBN-13: 978-1-946517-03-6
ISBN-10: 1-946517-03-8

To my mom
For your unconditional love and unwavering belief
that I can accomplish anything.
Love you!

ONE

"COME on, baby, just a little bit more."

Kat Bennett's body strained, and her arms shook as she pleaded with the stubborn iron rod in her hands. Who knew lug nuts could be so tight? Getting them off at home would've been a lot easier, but she hadn't noticed anything wrong when she'd left this morning. It took the stomach-dropping, telltale thumping of a flat tire for her to realize the powers that be still enjoyed a good laugh at her expense.

She was stuck, her cell phone battery drained, along a deserted two-lane road on a blisteringly hot Wisconsin afternoon. The stagnant humid air clung to her skin, sweat dripped down her face, and mosquitos buzzed around her ears. Figured she would get a flat tire on the hottest frickin' day of the summer.

Even though she'd only been stranded for half an hour, the hundred-degree heat index and her wrestling match with the iron-willed lug nuts had sent both her temperature and her temper into the red zone.

Thanks to the step-by-step directions in her owner's manual, she'd managed to locate the spare tire and figured out how to use the jack. It ticked her off that she'd gotten as far as lifting Bruno—her aging black Buick—six inches off the ground but couldn't budge the damn lug nuts. And the realization that a big, brawny guy could probably do it in a few seconds *really* ticked her off.

Kat blew the mosquitos from her face, tightened her grip on the smooth tire iron, and braced her feet in the gravel. Redoubling her efforts, she threw every ounce of her one hundred and five pounds into the job. When she failed to budge the damn thing a fraction of an inch, she dropped to her butt and cursed vividly.

Yesterday, Bruno's air conditioner had died. The day before that, she'd gotten a ticket for going a perfectly reasonable speed—in her opinion—and now this. Couldn't the universe give her one frickin' day without some sort of drama, complication, or issue?

She tensed at the sound of a vehicle approaching from the opposite direction. Sitting between her car and the grassy ditch, she couldn't see the type of car, but the engine's low purr suggested the sort of sports car usually favored by men. Her heart knocked in her chest when she heard its tires crunch over the gravel as it pulled onto the shoulder across the road.

"No, no, no," she mumbled to herself. "Don't stop. Please, don't stop."

This was the first person to even slow down. Not that there'd been many cars. Few took the scenic route to Sheboygan, the nearest "big town" to

Silver Bay. Most drivers opted for the highway a few miles to the west that ran parallel to the narrow, winding road she'd chosen on her trip home from one of the many responsibilities she'd unwittingly accumulated over the past few weeks.

In all fairness, she'd hidden from view the few times other cars had passed by, so the drivers had probably assumed there was no one stranded to help. Logically, she knew anyone who stopped would likely be a friendly Silver Bay resident. But she still felt trapped and vulnerable.

She used to be strong and fearless. Now she cowered.

God, that pissed her off.

Kat flipped from her butt to her hands and knees. Ignoring the bite of the gravel digging into her skin, she peered under Bruno's back end. Her mouth went dry and her pulse beat heavy in her throat as a set of male feet stepped from a low-slung red car.

She needed to find a weapon in case the guy wasn't a kind local. Scanning the ground, she spotted the tire iron. She snatched up the heavy rod and stood, holding her impromptu weapon along the length of her leg. No sense swinging for the bleachers if her visitor turned out to be friend rather than foe.

One look at him and the certainty of trouble slammed into her.

He stood well over six feet tall—his broad, muscular physique at least doubling her own weight. His surfer-boy blond hair, deep tan, and the stubble on his sculpted jaw made it clear he didn't spend his time in an office. A smile played around his full mouth as she met his gorgeous blue eyes. He bordered on perfection. And dammit, for some inexplicable reason that pissed her off even more than her weakness had moments ago.

"Heard you were in town." Kat kept her voice flat and her expression bored. No way would she let Logan McCabe realize how much he got to her.

"Arrived a week ago. Been hoping to see you around." His eyes lit with good-natured humor. "Nice to see you again. We miss you at La Vida, darl." His favorite term of endearment and his tantalizing Australian accent shot a hot jolt of awareness straight to her good parts.

Seriously? Why could her body never behave around this guy?

Last winter, she'd spent a month at La Vida de Ensueño, an environmentally friendly, socially responsible resort in Costa Rica that her brother, Paxton, owned. At first, Kat hadn't wanted to leave the natural beauty, friendly people, and sense of purpose she'd found at La Vida. But her attraction to Logan, her brother's best friend and the resort's reigning Casanova, had eventually convinced her otherwise.

Too big, too flirty, too tempting, too much trouble. Within moments of meeting him, Kat had summed him up with those four too's. She'd tried her damnedest to ignore him. Which worked about as well as trying to ignore a tornado hovering at the edge of her peripheral vision. Even when she managed to not look at him, she always knew he was there and could turn her world upside down without even noticing.

"It's nice to hear I've been missed," she said, "but I can't imagine Pax and Sage coming up for air long enough to notice I'm gone."

Logan grinned. "True. Those two are in their own little world. The rest of us miss you though. You lived there for five or six months before leaving, ay?"

"One," she snarled, shoving back dark strands of hair that had escaped from her ponytail. *Un-frickin'-believable.* He'd haunted every day of her stay at La Vida, and the jerkface didn't even have a clue how long she'd spent there.

"Huh." He shrugged. "Seemed longer."

She did a mental eye roll, then took in the low-riding black boardshorts and the stretchy blue swim shirt clinging so tightly that his chest resembled a detailed topographic map. His body had more hills, bluffs, and ridges than the Driftless Area National Wildlife Refuge.

Too damn hot. Adding another "too" to her list, she resisted fanning herself with her own hand.

"Going surfing?" Kat asked. While his outfit made it obvious he was headed for a swim, the board strapped to the roof explained why he was on the road to Sheboygan.

"Yip. Heard the funny sounding town south of here is the 'Malibu of the Midwest.' Had to give it a go." His gaze dropped to her flat tire. "Need a hand?"

"Nope. Almost done here."

He shifted his baby blues from the flat tire still firmly attached to Bruno and studied her with a look of skeptical intrigue. "Lug nuts stuck?"

"No." Okay, maybe she'd snapped the reply a little too quickly in retrospect. But how the hell had he figured that out?

"Time for you to leave." She motioned for him to go with a few backward flicks of her fingers. "Buh-bye."

"Sorry, can't leave until you do." He gestured to the tire iron she was white-knuckling in her right hand. "Now are you going take a swing at me with that thing or use it to get your tire off?"

She glared for a long moment. "Not sure. Maybe both."

"Fair enough. Let me know when you decide." Logan began whistling a happy little tune and rocked back on his heels, looking around the tree-lined road with an expression of casual interest.

The bastard.

Kat grunted, spun on her heel, and shoved the end of the two-foot rod onto one of the stubborn lug nuts with a little more force than necessary. No way would she let him change the damn tire. She *so* did not need his help. She gripped the rod, scrunched her eyes closed, and started to compose a little mental prayer to Hercules.

"One time," Logan said, interrupting her plea to the Greek hero, "I watched my mum change a tire when I was an ankle-biter. She angled the tire iron so that it came off the lug nut at about eleven o'clock, with the nut as the clock's center. Then she turned around and stepped onto the tire iron with all her weight. It was an ace move."

Damn. That might actually work.

Without looking back, Kat adjusted the wrench to the correct angle, straightened, took a deep breath, and stepped up and onto the lever with her right heel. In one smooth motion, the tire iron gently lowered to the ground. *Yes!* Flying high from success, she quickly loosened the other nuts, removed the flat tire, and slipped on the new one. Minutes later, she tightened the spare tire into place and lowered Bruno back to the ground.

While Logan watched the whole process, he never tried to take over. She had to give him credit. Her petite size usually made guys try to do everything for her. Which, of course, ticked her off.

She put the last tool into the trunk and slammed it shut in triumph. With a quick bubble of laughter, she turned to Logan. "I did it!" Her smile dropped at his look of sharp interest. "What?" she demanded.

"First time you've ever really smiled at me," he said, his accent thicker than usual.

Locked in his intense gaze, she remained motionless, unsure if she wanted to remember, ruin, or ignore the moment.

A few heavy breaths later, he grinned and shook his head as if breaking from a trance. "Blinded me for a minute."

His words sent an unwanted wave of warmth and desire through her. *Ugh*. She had to put an end to the weird connection that started building between them at La Vida. Time to slip back into her edgy 'tude.

"You're full of shit, Logan. Now get the hell out of here before I change my mind and start beating you with that tire iron after all."

He laughed and lifted his hands in a palms-out, no-harm-meant gesture. "I'm sensing some hostility."

She crossed her arms and cocked an eyebrow. "What tipped you off?"

"The repeated threats of violence mostly." He

tilted his head and studied her. "What is it about me that gets you so worked up, darl?"

Fighting back the growl building in her throat, Kat drew in a breath and narrowed her eyes. "Well, I won't use the phrase 'manwhore' because—"

"Think you just did," he interrupted.

"Because," she repeated more firmly, "I'm sure there's never been an exchange of money. But I can't respect a guy who changes women more often than I change shoes."

"It's not like I sleep with a different woman every night."

"Maybe. But you don't stick. When's the last time you dated anyone longer than a month?"

"Long-term isn't my specialty." Logan shrugged. "I'm sure you can relate."

"Relate? How?" Kat demanded. "I don't bounce from bed to bed."

"Sure of that? In the last year you've moved from DC to Silver Bay to Costa Rica where you stayed with Sage, then Pax, then Susanna before moving back to Silver Bay again. That's a lot more beds than I've slept in."

"I slept in those beds alone," she said between clenched teeth. "You didn't."

"And that upsets you?"

"Of course not," she snapped. "I couldn't care less who you sleep with."

"Doesn't this entire conversation prove otherwise?"

Kat threw her hands in the air. "God, you're exhausting!"

Logan flashed a boyish smile. "Thanks."

She growled in frustration and pointed down the

road. "We're done here. Thanks for stopping. Now leave."

He dipped his head in mock concession. "All right, all right. I'll go." He crossed back to his car and opened the driver's door. "You're heading home, right?"

"Yep. Straight home. No problem. Got it covered. Buh-bye."

He climbed into his car. "I'll follow you to make sure that spare tire holds." He slammed the door shut before she could respond.

No frickin' way. She did not need him hovering over her like some paranoid helicopter parent on the playground.

"No thanks," she yelled over the sound of his car's engine purring to life. "Don't follow me. Just go surfing." She gestured dramatically in the direction of Sheboygan with both hands like an overenthusiastic ground's crewman at the airport.

Logan revved the engine. "Can't hear you," he mouthed through the window, cupping a hand behind his ear. He added a wolfish smile capable of melting the panties off any mortal woman.

"Fine. Whatever," she muttered, tempted to kick the tire. Or him. Logan always did whatever the hell he wanted anyway.

She stormed into her driver's seat. It totally pissed her off that he was right about how his behavior could get her "so worked up." Her last week in Costa Rica served as an excellent case in point. When a group of youngish women checked into La Vida itching to celebrate some sort of minor career accomplishment, Logan had taken it upon himself to make sure they had the time of their lives.

Kat had spent a teeth-grinding week watching him hit on anything with two legs and a pair of breasts. She'd managed to keep her irritation to herself—for the most part at least—until the night she saw him walking toward one of the villas with a giggling woman on each arm and an infuriating grin on his face.

That's when she'd lost it. The details were thankfully a little fuzzy—blinding rage could apparently do that to a person—but Kat did remember storming to her villa, throwing her stuff into a suitcase, and booking a ticket back to Silver Bay. Sure, she had no claim on Logan, but she'd been instantly attracted to him in Costa Rica. Watching the asshole take two women to bed was more than she could stand.

Kat continued her mental rant about him for most of the drive home. At least her irritation with Logan kept her from thinking about the talk her parents wanted to have with her tonight. She had a pretty good idea what the "talk" would be about, and she wasn't looking forward to another grilling. Not that she had much of a choice. Except for the month at La Vida last winter, she'd been living with them at her childhood home since moving back from Washington, DC almost a year ago.

Tonight would be another one of the heart-to-hearts her folks insisted on having every few months. *Why did you quit your job? Why did you leave DC? What are you going to do with your life now? Why keep floating from job to job? Why have you been even more distracted since leaving Costa Rica?* Blah. Blah. Blah.

No way in hell she'd tell anyone the real reason she'd quit her DC job and moved home to Silver

Bay, least of all her overprotective parents.

Kat turned down the tree-lined drive to their estate and parked Bruno in one of the extra spaces beside the four-car garage on the left side of the sprawling lakefront house. She tipped her head from side to side and enjoyed the rewarding cracking of her neck. Then she blew out a breath and plastered on a smile.

Time to put on her game face.

She hopped out of her car, hoping to make it inside before Logan arrived. At least he hadn't been tailing her that closely, but she knew he'd show up sooner or later. Even though he had his share of flaws, Logan genuinely liked to help people. Hopefully, once he saw her car parked by the garage he'd continue around the circular drive and head right back out on the road and away from her.

She hustled to the side door. The thick, humid air clung to her and added another layer of yuck to her already filthy skin. She glanced at the clock on her phone and groaned. Her little tire-changing adventure had eaten into the time she'd allotted for showering before dinner. Guess hot-and-sweaty would be her look for this family meeting.

The moment she stepped into the mudroom her parents' three-year-old golden retriever, Cosmo, bounded toward her with one of his many stuffed animals gripped in his mouth.

"Hey, buddy. Did you miss me today?" Kat kneeled to pet his head and received multiple licks to the face.

Cosmo's whole body wagged with excitement. Every time she walked through the door, his jubilant, better-than-Christmas-morning reaction made her feel like a superstar. Sure would be nice if everyone greeted her with that kind of enthusiasm.

Kat dropped a quick kiss on his smooth head. "Sorry, boy. I have to clean up. I promise to give you some extra belly rubs later."

She moved into the half bath attached to the mudroom, washed the grease from her hands, splashed cold water on her face, and redid her ponytail. "Good as it's going to get," she said into the mirror.

A moment before she rounded the corner into the kitchen, she heard her parents enter the room from the other side.

"She's going to be insulted," her mom said.

"I'm aware of that, but she can't live here any longer," her dad replied, conviction filling his voice. "She walked away from a promising career in international affairs for no apparent reason. She's twenty-eight years old, doesn't have a job, and lives with her parents."

Her mom sighed. "Maybe she needs a little more time."

"It has been almost a year since she left DC and almost five months since she got back from Costa Rica. I am happy to help our children when they are trying to make something of themselves, but Katherine isn't even trying. We cannot enable this behavior any longer. It's time for her to move forward with her life." Her dad's voice shook with frustration. "I don't understand when she got so damn lazy!"

Kat's gut clenched, and her heart pounded. Shame washed through her, flooding her eyes with tears. God, she wanted her old life back. She wanted to feel strong again even if it had only been a false sense of strength. Ignorance truly was bliss. One mistake had taught her the truth. She was weak. And even if she hid her cowardice from everyone else, that truth would always haunt her.

Pushing back the hurt, she tipped her chin up and stepped into the kitchen doorway before she had to hear any more about the loser she'd become. "No worries," she said in a neutral voice. "I'm happy to find somewhere else to live."

Her parents flinched and turned to look at her.

"Kat, honey. We didn't know you were there." Her mom took a step forward, her face tight with concern.

Kat extended her hand to stop her. "It's fine. Dad's right. I am too old to live at home. Probably best if I look for somewhere else to stay tonight."

She turned and stumbled out of the house, desperate to leave before they saw the tears threatening to spill down her cheeks. She'd meant what she'd said—she was too old to live with her parents.

Problem was, she was too damn afraid to live alone.

•••

Crouched next to Kat's car, Logan inspected the dilapidated spare tire. The minute he'd seen that piece of shit spare, he'd known it didn't have much life left. That's one of the reasons he'd insisted on following her home. Looked like she'd made it to her parents' house just in time. He could almost see the last of the air leak from the tire as the car slowly sank closer to the ground. He grimaced. Two flat tires in one day was pretty damn unlucky.

Still at tire level, he heard rather than saw the side door of the house open and slam shut. Both the soft, hurried footsteps heading his way and his own instincts told him it was Kat. His senses always heightened and heated when she was near.

Since the day he'd met her, he'd been drawn to her. A tiny little thing, Kat looked to be more than a foot shorter and a hundred pounds lighter than him. Her small size and expressive blue-gray eyes had always triggered in him the desire to take care of her, but he'd gotten his hand slapped—figuratively and literally—on more than one occasion for trying to help her when she didn't want or need it.

She reminded him of a roaring fire—beautiful, strong, hypnotic. And like a fire, he knew she'd burn him if he ever got too close. So he teased but never touched.

Besides, Pax would kick his arse—or at least try to—if Logan became involved with his little sister. Not that he blamed Pax. Logan didn't do long-term, and they both knew it.

When he heard her footsteps reach the back corner of the car, he slowly straightened to his full height.

The moment she saw him, she screamed and leapt back.

"What the hell, Logan!" She wrapped trembling arms tightly around her slender body and glared at him. "You scared me."

Her skin's usual golden tone had drained to white, her wide-set eyes bright with fear and anger.

"Sorry, darl. I didn't mean to scare you. Just

checking your tire. Looks like your spare wasn't up to the job. You've got another flat."

"No frickin' way?" Kat stepped closer to look at the spare, irritation replacing the fear in her eyes.

"Rough day."

"You don't even know," she mumbled and shook her head.

"Let's drop off your full-size tire at the shop in town and grab dinner while they patch it. You can fill me in on small-town America living since I'm going to be here for the summer." He motioned to her car. "After dinner, we can swing back here and get you up and running for good."

She blew out a long breath of defeat. "Yeah. Okay."

"Careful. Your lack of enthusiasm could really hurt my ego."

She snorted. "Big guy, a sledgehammer couldn't dent your ego."

TWO

KAT grabbed her purse from the mudroom—yes, she'd made her grand escape without thinking about a wallet or keys—and opened the trunk. Before she could stop him, Logan lifted her original flat tire out of the back and carried it in one hand to his own trunk. He was so damn big it looked like he was toting a life ring rather than a full-size tire. Next to him, she probably looked like a puny, pint-sized princess who couldn't take care of herself.

She huffed her way to the passenger side of his car and slid into the seat. "I could have carried the tire, you know."

"Yeah, I know."

"Then why'd you do it?"

Logan shrugged as he began driving the short distance to Silver Bay's small commercial area. "It feels good to help people."

"Whatever, Superman." Kat was totally unwilling to bond with him over anything, even though she'd thought that exact thing when she was mowing a lawn in the blazing sun just a few hours ago.

Not long after returning from Costa Rica, she had unintentionally become the Jill-of-all-trades for a group of older widows in the area. It had started the day she ran into her childhood piano teacher, Ruth Dobolek, at the Silver Bay Market. Mrs. Dobolek had lost her husband to cancer and now had a small home near the center of town to take care of by herself. Kat had ended up carrying Mrs. Dobolek's groceries home for her that afternoon and every Wednesday afternoon since.

After that, Kat had helped Mrs. D and two of her friends, Lillian and Margaret, with tasks that were easy for the young but potentially dangerous for the elderly. She'd hung bird feeders, mowed lawns, brought items down from the attic, taken other items up to the attic, hung window treatments, carried large bags of cat food into the house, and any other chore they could find for her.

Somehow within the last few months, one good deed had snowballed into a nearly full-time—albeit completely non-paying—job.

"Turn here." She pointed to a freestanding shop at the edge of town with a freshly paved parking lot, small reception area, and six large garage doors running down the side of the building.

Danny's Tires, Brakes, and More was owned by Danny Sullivan, her onetime classmate. Though he'd crushed on her through high school, she'd ignored all the signs of his affection. No sense in ruining a friendship over unreturned adolescent hormones.

Kat climbed from the car and strode into the shop. Logan followed at a leisurely pace.

"You could have stayed in the car," she said

dryly as they entered.

"I need to get a feel for the community. Can't meet any locals if I stay in the car."

"Fine. But I'll do the talking."

She glanced around and spotted Danny behind the counter. He used to be a string bean in high school. Now he was tall and lean with kind brown eyes and a welcoming smile.

"Hey, Kat." He looked over her shoulder at Logan and then out the front window at Logan's sports car. "Did you finally let your dad buy you a new ride?"

"Nah, it's his." She jerked her thumb behind her. "Bruno's got a flat. Any chance you can patch it?"

"Sure. I can get to it tomorrow."

"Let me rephrase my question. Any chance you can drop everything and immediately patch a tire for the girl who got you a date to senior prom?"

He raised an eyebrow, trying to look stern, but the smile tugging at his lips ruined the effect. "I wanted to go to prom with you."

She flashed him a grin. "Well, that was stupid. Mindy had a much bigger rack and was known for putting out. You should be grateful. Maybe even grateful enough to get my tire fixed within the hour, don't you think?"

"You're a pain in the ass."

"Is that a yes?"

He sighed. "You know it is."

"Great. Thanks, Danny. I'll be back."

"Is that a promise or a threat?" he asked as she turned to leave the shop with Logan tailing close behind.

"Bit of both," she threw over her shoulder on

her way out the door.

As one of Danny's employees unloaded her tire from Logan's trunk, Kat mentally checked "get tire fixed" off her to-do list. Progress was being made, but she needed to hurry things up if she was going to find a place to stay tonight before it got dark. After her dad's summary of her pathetic state, she couldn't bear to spend another night at her parents' house.

Besides, living with her parents for almost a year had taken a toll on her self-respect. She'd been raised on stories of how her father, Richard Bennett, had turned his father's small family cabinet company into a national brand. The realization that she'd become the loser daughter living off her parents' wealth really pissed her off. God, she didn't want to be that person, but she didn't know how to beat back the unrelenting fear clouding, controlling, and distorting her life.

"Where to next?" Logan asked, falling in step beside her.

"I need to swing by Hannah's place before we grab a bite to eat. We can leave your car here. It's only a few blocks to the town square."

Her sister Hannah owned a coffee shop called Fresh. It served delicious pastries and coffee for breakfast and sandwiches, salads, and soups for lunch. Hannah lived above the storefront in an adorable apartment. The apartment was small, but Kat knew Hannah would let her sleep there for a couple of nights while she searched for a longer-term place to live. Her other sister Claire had a bigger place, but she also had two kids.

"Sure." Logan nodded and began walking beside her down the block. "I like Hannah. I met her when

I first got to town. She's one of the nice sisters."

"Agreed." She laughed and turned to look up at him. "But I'm the fun one."

Logan's eyes darkened. "I like fun."

Her belly tightened, and her wayward nipples perked up in interest. She should know better than to flirt with the world's biggest player. Bantering with guys had always been her thing, but this strong physical attraction to Logan threw her off her game and messed with her head.

To cut the sudden and unwanted tension, she rolled her eyes so dramatically she almost lost her balance. "Cool your jets, big guy. Dessert is the most fun you're getting out of me tonight. Come on. Less talk, more walk."

Ugh. Why Logan? Why did she get all hot and bothered about a guy who moved through women quick enough to make her head spin?

She might be flirtatious, but she'd never been easy. Hell, she'd only ever slept with three guys. And all of them had been semi-serious boyfriends at the time. She didn't do one-night stands.

Even so, Logan's tantalizing proximity intensified everything. Her heart raced, and her nerve endings tingled. Each breath filled her lungs with the scent of soap rising from his sun-warmed skin and conjured images of slick bodies and tangled sheets.

Pushing that thought from her mind, she looked across Main Street to the darkened windows above her sister's coffee shop.

"Oh, frick," she mumbled as her gut twisted into a knot. "I forgot. Hannah went to Chicago with Claire and the kids."

"When is she back?"

"Not until tomorrow." Kat remained frozen on the sidewalk, her pulse beating in her throat. It would be dark in less than two hours, and neither of her sisters were home to ask for refuge. "I need a place to stay, and I knew either Hannah or Claire would let me crash on their couch for a couple of nights."

"I thought you were living at your parents' place?"

Kat cringed, fidgeted with a ring on her finger, and avoided eye contact. "No longer an option. Long story."

"You can tell me about it over a beer." He placed his hand on the small of her back and guided her across the square to the entrance of Bayside, the town's best bar and grill.

When he opened the door for her, she fought back the rising anxiety over her homelessness and took a deep breath. Turning left inside, she hustled through Bayside's bar, marched through the crowded tables in the next room, and slid into the lone open booth along the window.

When Logan settled into the seat across from her, she handed him a menu.

"You in a hurry?" he asked, one eyebrow raised.

"Sorry to rush you. But it's getting late, and I have nowhere to sleep tonight. It's summer. The hotel in town will be full."

"My place has two bedrooms. You can stay with me." He shrugged and opened the menu. "Are the burgers good here?"

Kat stared at him, mouth open, and tipped her head to the side. "You can't possibly think that's a good idea."

"Why not?" He grinned over the menu. "A burger sounds ace."

"Not the burger, big guy. I'm talking about me crashing at your place. Bad idea."

"Afraid you won't be able to resist me?"

"I can resist you."

"You sure? I can be very persuasive."

"Tell you what. If I feel myself start to weaken, I'll just ask you to tell me the full name, eye color, and favorite food of the last three women you've slept with." Kat leveled him with her I've-got-your-number stare. "Your inability to answer those questions should douse any lustful thoughts."

"I might surprise you."

"Fine." She shrugged. "I bet you can't even tell me the names of those two blond guests you paraded off to bed with at the resort."

His eyes widened in surprise. "Who?"

Kat bit back an expletive. Then she took a deep breath, willed her blood pressure under control, and did a slow count to five. "I rest my case."

"Hate to ruin the playboy image you've created for me, but I've never slept with any of La Vida's guests."

She snorted. "I saw you leading two of those women from Georgia to their villa like the frickin' Pied Piper of one-night stands." Kat crossed her arms and glared. "I'm not buying that look of confused innocence for a second."

Logan's lips twitched and laughter danced in his bright blue eyes as he closed the menu and slowly slid it to the edge of the table. "South Carolina, not Georgia," he said patiently, as if explaining basic geography to a child. "Jennifer and Jackie were from

South Carolina. And I didn't sleep with them. They'd had a few too many glasses of wine that night, and Jennifer kept talking about taking a dip in the ocean, which would have been a very bad idea in their condition. So I made sure they got to their villa safely, then hung around at the beach until I was sure they'd gone to bed. I would have explained it to you earlier if I'd known you were jealous." He winked and offered her a wolfish smile.

"Sorry to disappoint you, big guy. My reaction to your friendly three-way was disgust, not jealousy. Even if I choose to believe you didn't sleep with those women, you're still a player, and from what I can tell, you're damn good at it. I, on the other hand, don't have time for games. I need to deal with real-life problems."

"Then solve one of your problems by staying at my place tonight, until your sisters get back."

The worry churning her stomach eased at the thought of sleeping in a room next to Logan's. Though he brought his own brand of trouble into her life, she felt safe with him.

Even her attraction to him didn't worry her much. She could resist Logan McCabe if it bought her time to find a longer-term solution to her housing dilemma.

"Okay. I'll stay tonight," she said with a resigned sigh. "Just don't read anything into this decision. I am not joining your long list of conquests tonight, so keep it in your pants. Capiche?"

Logan's grin widened, and his eyes brightened with restrained laughter. "Fair enough. I'll make you a promise. I won't take *it* out of my pants until you ask me to."

"Until?" Kat snorted. "You're a cocky guy, Logan. And honestly, I kinda like that about you." She shrugged and flipped open her menu. "But just to be clear, there's no chance in hell that's ever gonna happen."

•••

After finishing their burgers and beers, they picked up her repaired tire from Danny's, and then headed to her parents' house to retrieve her car. For speed's sake, Kat agreed to let him change the tire while she slipped into the house to pack an overnight bag.

Okay, yes, earlier she'd forgotten that too. In her defense, though, she had expected to stay with Hannah or Claire, who would have gladly loaned her whatever she needed.

Thankfully, she didn't see her parents and assumed they were on their nightly post-dinner walk along the beach. On her way out the door, she stopped in the kitchen and left a note explaining that she'd found a place to stay and would be back for the rest of her things later in the week. She didn't know where the frick she'd be taking those things, but, hey, she preferred to be upbeat.

By the time she stepped out of the air-conditioned house into the humid evening air—a mere ten minutes later—Logan was already stowing the spare tire and tools back into Bruno's trunk.

"You're already done?" Kat asked a little impressed.

He turned toward her and winked. "I'm good with my hands."

She sighed, tipped her head to the side, and gave

him a look of mock sadness. "You really can't shut it off, can you?"

"Nope," he answered cheerfully. "Now, are you ready to spend the night at my place? We can go skinny-dipping to cool down from this heat wave. It's really secluded, so no worries about privacy."

She blew out a breath. "Just drive. I'll follow you in Bruno."

"Bruno?"

"Yeah. My car, Bruno the Buick."

He cocked an eyebrow. "Your car's name is Bruno the Buick?"

"Bruno for short."

Logan eyed her for a moment, then shrugged. "Good-oh." He climbed into his car and shut the door.

Kat slid behind Bruno's wheel and tossed her overnight bag onto the passenger seat. She didn't know what the hell "good-oh" meant but figured it was easier to just run with it than to ask for an explanation. Plus, there was only an hour or so of daylight left, and she preferred to get settled into his place before darkness arrived.

She followed Logan from her parents' estate, heading north along the shore. After twenty minutes on the winding road, he turned onto a long, narrow drive leading toward the lake. The drive curved through tall trees for a hundred yards or so before ending at an adorable cottage with off-white siding, two dormer windows, and a prime location thirty yards from the sandy shore of Lake Michigan.

Gravel crunched under her tires as she slowed to a stop next to the cottage. She grabbed her stuff and climbed from the car. Looked like Logan hadn't been kidding about the house's seclusion. She almost reached back inside for the heavy metal flashlight in her glove box.

Thankfully, she wouldn't be here alone tonight.

"Where's your closest neighbor?"

"About a half mile farther north. The family that owns this place also owns most of the acreage surrounding it. Apparently, they consider it an investment."

"Smart. Lakefront property is valuable." Kat drew in a deep breath of rich summer air, hoping it would steady her nerves.

The mingled scents of cut grass and the lakeshore flooded her with memories of childhood—memories of evenings with her family, swimming in the lake or chasing fireflies barefoot in the backyard. Even the low, steady hum of the cottage's air conditioner and the faint sound of waves washing onto shore reminded her of the time when fear didn't control her life.

"How did you find this place?" she asked.

"Your mum set it up."

"She wants you to help add a social outreach component to her charity like the one at La Vida, right?"

"Yip."

"How are you going to do that? This is Silver Bay, not Costa Rica." Kat shook her head. "There are different needs here."

"I just have to find where the greatest need for help is and go from there." Logan extended his right hand, inviting her to lead the way to the front door.

"Good luck with that," Kat mumbled. Bag slung over her shoulder, she headed for the cottage.

Logan followed only a few steps away. He moved quietly for such a big guy. Not that she needed to hear him to know he was close. Every nerve ending in her body hummed in awareness whenever he was within a mile radius.

She climbed the two front steps and stepped aside for him to unlock the door.

"Go on. It's open."

Unbelievable. "You didn't lock up before you left?" She looked over her shoulder, one eyebrow raised in accusation.

"Nah. Didn't seem like a rough neighborhood."

Kat huffed and shook her head. She vaguely remembered what it felt like living life unafraid, and she'd give anything to feel that way again. Maybe if she spent enough time with Logan some of his casual "no worries" attitude would rub off on her.

Stepping into the entranceway, she scanned the cottage's interior. To her right was an airy kitchen with white cabinets, stainless appliances, and a large island with barstools tucked under the overhanging granite countertop. Pine floors spread through the kitchen and into the living room which held two clean-lined leather chairs and a stone-colored couch. An old wooden trunk with rusted metal latches and a lot of character served as the coffee table for the cozy room. The best feature, however, was the wall of windows running along the far side, showing off a screened-in porch and an impressive view of Lake Michigan.

"This place is gorgeous. You sure you're going to want to leave at the end of the summer?" Kat asked.

Logan walked into the kitchen, grabbed two beers from the fridge, and twisted both caps off.

"No worries. It's harder for me to stay in one place than it is to leave. After spending a few years in Costa Rica, I reckon it's time I wander for a while." He offered her a bottle.

"Thanks." She accepted the beer and took a sip. "So you don't stick with anything, huh?"

Logan stiffened and looked at her with a serious expression she'd never seen from him before. "What do you mean?"

"I knew you walked away from the women in your life without a backwards glance. I didn't know you left places and friends so easily too. Pax, Brick, and the rest of La Vida's staff are more like family than coworkers. I'm surprised you're willing to desert them."

Logan shrugged. "I'm not deserting anyone. I can stay in touch. Just feels like it's time to move on."

She tipped her head to the side. "Why the itchy feet? Afraid you might care about someone or something if you invest too much of your time?"

His mouth curved into a humorless smile. "You're a real tiger, aren't you?"

"Can be. And you didn't answer my question."

"I thought it was rhetorical."

"Good point. No need to tell me what I already know." Kat eyed the room again, this time dramatically craning her neck around. "Where the hell is my room? We've spent a lot of time together today. I'd better give you some space before you start feeling the need to make a break for it."

Logan chuckled and pointed to the left as humor returned to his eyes. "Around the corner. There's only one bathroom so we've got to share."

"Got it, big guy. Thanks for letting me crash here tonight." She started walking in the direction he'd indicated.

"You're welcome. And Kat … ?" He waited until she stopped and turned back to look at him. "No need to change out of your nightie before brekkie in the morning. It won't bother me. I'm rather open-minded.

"I know. That's my second favorite thing about you."

"Second? What's the first?"

She grinned and slowly scanned down and then up his long, hard physique. When she reached his eyes, she moaned out a small sigh. "I think you already know. Goodnight, Logan."

Turning on her heel, she grinned at the shocked expression on his handsome face. Giddy pride swept through her. She'd just left the world's biggest flirt speechless.

Smart? No, probably not. Enjoyable? Yes, definitely.

Kat walked into the nautical-themed guest room and shut the door firmly behind her. After turning on the small bedside lamp and double checking the window locks, she began unpacking her overnight bag, a goofy grin still on her face. She'd take small victories where she could.

Tomorrow she could worry about finding a place to live and getting a real job. And maybe soon she'd even figure out a way to become the strong, independent kick-ass girl she used to be.

THREE

SHORTLY before sunrise, Kat crept to the kitchen in search of coffee. The fancy coffee machine with its impressive—if slightly surprising—selection of flavored pods made her send up a silent thank you to the gods of java. She loved rising early to enjoy the stillness of daybreak, but without her coffee, mornings could get ugly.

Daybreak without coffee was like watching a movie with her favorite hottie actor, Carter O'Reilly, cast as the bad guy: unpleasant, unnatural, and fundamentally wrong on every level.

After brewing a quick cup, she tiptoed to the screened-in porch and settled into the large outdoor-style sectional with deep red cushions. A cool breeze blew through the screens, bringing a nice reprieve from the heat wave of the past week. Curling her feet under her, she set her coffee mug on the arm of the sofa and sent a quick text to Claire, her ever-efficient and loved-by-everyone oldest sister.

Kat was the baby of the family, while Claire—

second born and the first of the three girls—was just eighteen months younger than Pax. Not only was Claire older and wiser, she was the Bennett kid who least resembled Kat in looks and temperament. Sure, they'd both inherited their mom's fair skin, but Claire was a natural blonde and had scored four extra inches in height over petite, dark-haired Kat. Those inches seemed to contribute to Claire's authoritative air. As an executive at Bennett Industries, her older sister had her pulse on Silver Bay. If anyone would know where to find a roommate at the height of summer tourist season, it would be Claire.

Thankfully Kat's phone vibrated with an incoming call before she stewed any longer about her vertical disadvantage. Grinning, she answered her phone. "How's Chicago?"

"Great," Claire said. "We all went to the aquarium yesterday. Today Grace and I are going to the American Girl store while Hannah takes Ty for a Divvy bike ride along the lake."

"Sounds fun. Sorry I'm not there with you guys," Kat said.

"That's okay. I understand that laundry day is important too."

Claire had asked both of her sisters to join her on the trip. Hannah had agreed instantly, but Kat had been afraid if she canceled on mowing Lillian's lawn, the eighty-something-year-old woman would have tried to do it herself in yesterday's killer heat.

"Uh. Yep. Laundry's super important," Kat mumbled with a cringe. Man, her excuse sounded even lamer hearing it from Claire.

"I'm just happy you have incorporated color back into your wardrobe. For a while there after you moved back, you looked like you were either in mourning or a biker gang."

"Had to give up the look in Costa Rica. Too damn hot there to wear black all the time." And after spending one week at La Vida, Kat hadn't felt like wearing head to toe black any longer, but she didn't feel like sharing that telling piece of information with her sister. "Anyway, I called because I'm hoping you can help me solve a little problem."

"What's wrong?" her sister asked, instantly alert.

"Mom and Dad kinda sorta kicked me out of the house yesterday. But it's okay," she quickly reassured. "I get it. I couldn't stay there forever. I know you or Hannah would let me sleep on your couch for a while, but I need to find a more permanent solution. Any idea of someone we know in Silver Bay who needs a roommate?"

"Why don't you rent a place on your own?"

"I don't have enough money to live by myself." The lie slipped off her tongue so easily she almost believed it herself.

"Mom and Dad would lend you money. Dad's always complaining that he wants to help more than any of us will let him."

"No way am I taking cash from Mom and Dad. I refuse to become the loser Bennett kid who needs her rich parents' money. It's bad enough I've been living with them. It's time I get a new job and an apartment."

Claire chuckled. "I work for Dad, and they cosigned Pax's loan for La Vida and Hannah's loan for Fresh. Heck, even Dad had help when he first started out. Grandpa *gave* him the company, remember? It's not a crime to accept help from your family."

Kat snorted. "You can't compare building careers and businesses to bankrolling my rent. I need a job and a roommate, not a loan from the parents."

"I get it, kiddo." Claire's voice softened with concern. "I just hate to see you struggle. Why don't you talk to Hannah? She mentioned needing help at the café. I'm sure she'd be happy to hire you."

"Good to know. I'll talk with her when you guys get back in town. Now, any ideas on where I can sleep tonight? And before you ask me, yes I *do* know how lucky I am to have such an amazing sister who's always willing to help my pathetic ass."

"You're not pathetic. You're just finding your footing, and I'm really ticked the parents threw you out yesterday. What the heck were they thinking? I'll call Dad and—" Claire stopped abruptly and sucked in air. "Wait a second. Where did you sleep last night?"

"Huh. Funny you ask." Kat pretended to yawn in a not-so-subtle stall tactic. "I ran into Logan McCabe yesterday, and he let me stay at his place."

"You mean our brother's best friend? The tall, incredibly hot blond guy from Australia? The one you claimed changes women more often than I change lip glosses? That Logan?"

"Yes." Kat thunked her phone against her forehead with each word. "The tall, incredibly hot blond guy from Australia. Thanks for that vivid description, by the way, like sleeping in a room next to him wasn't already hard enough."

Claire's laughter filled her ear. "Kiddo, I expect plenty of women in Silver Bay would be happy to trade places. Logan's caused quite a stir since he arrived. You should stay right where you are until he either physically removes you or the cops issue a restraining order."

"I can't stay here," she hissed.

"Why not?"

"First, he only invited me to stay for one night. Second, I made a really big deal about being able to resist him. And there's a slight chance I overstated my abilities on that one."

"Fantastic! This could be just the jump-start you need to get things going again in your dating life too."

"Logan isn't a long-term kind of guy."

"Even better. Relationships get more difficult the longer they last. Enjoy the blinding attraction and passionate sex now, then get out before either of you is stupid enough to try to make it permanent."

"Yikes. Bitter much?

"Not bitter, realistic."

"Okay, then your version of reality is kinda bitter. Aren't you the romantic in the family?" Kat asked.

"Not anymore," her sister said. "And you're missing the point. I love the life I share with my kiddos. I wouldn't change it up for anything. But I wish I would have enjoyed myself a little more before having children. It would be nice to have one wild, passionate fling to look back on fondly."

"Guess I never thought of it that way." Kat sipped her coffee and watched hues of orange spread across the sky as the sun rose from the water.

"So you'll have sex with the hunky Australian?" Claire asked, all business.

Kat choked on her coffee.

"You okay?"

"Fine, fine," Kat sputtered out between coughs.

"Doesn't sound like it. Should I call nine-one-one? Oh, I know! You should ask Logan to give you mouth to mouth."

"Hanging up now." Kat ended the call and tossed her phone onto the cushion beside her.

Had her practical sister actually encouraged her to have a fling with a major-league player? She had to admit the unexpected advice intrigued her.

Hell, the more she thought about it, the real crime seemed like *not* having sex with a gorgeous guy when they were both single, healthy adults. Decades from now, maybe memories of wild monkey sex with Logan would put a smile on her old, wrinkled face.

Holy shit. She could talk herself into anything.

Kat gave her head a quick shake. Claire's advice had twisted her thoughts to the point that right seemed like left, up seemed like down, and down seemed like a really, really good idea.

"Good morning, tiger."

She jumped at the sound of Logan's voice. She narrowed her eyes as she turned her head and saw him, shiny with sweat, standing outside on the stairs leading from the beach to the enclosed deck. The moment he stepped through the screen door, the air thickened and the spacious area seemed to shrink. His black running shorts and red T-shirt clung to mouthwatering muscles. And she wasn't being corny or overly dramatic. Her mouth literally watered from looking at him.

"I thought you were still sleeping," she said, her voice slightly strangled.

"Nah. Just got back from a run along the beach. I haven't been able to find a decent gym in town."

"Just got back?" Kat repeated his words as a question in attempt to clarify how long he'd been standing on the steps.

A wolfish smile was his only response.

Holy hell. How much had he heard?

"I've been thinking," Logan said.

"Sounds dangerous."

His smile widened as he took a seat on the other side of the sectional. He leaned back and kicked his feet up on the low wrought-iron coffee table. He looked content, carefree, and gorgeous as sin.

The sudden image of her straddling him on the sectional flashed through her mind and sent a wave of longing spiraling south. She gritted her teeth and took a deep breath. Damn Claire for planting the idea of a steamy fling in her mind. Kat had enough things to deal with right now. She didn't need to add fighting sexual fantasies to the list.

"I'm staying here for free," Logan said. "Part of the job perks. You're welcome to crash with me this summer while you look for a job and a more permanent place to live."

"Won't I get in the way of your social life?"

"I don't plan to bring women here, if that's what you mean."

"Keeping the Batcave's location on the down low, huh?" She clicked her tongue and winked in a conspiratorial manner. "Smart move."

"Something like that." He glanced at the techie-looking watch strapped to his wrist. A slight frown marred his features as he stood up. "I gotta go. Let me know what you decide."

36

"Commissioner Gordon need you?"

"First Superman, now Batman. It's ace you think of me as a superhero, darl." He shot her a cocky smile as he walked past her and into the kitchen.

"Smug bastard," Kat muttered, rolling her eyes. He would be an even bigger pain in the ass if she told him he looked like Thor. Guess she would have to keep that little nugget to herself.

She sipped her coffee and considered her options. If she turned down Logan's offer, she would have to spend the day frantically looking for somewhere else to stay. And, if she didn't find anywhere by tonight, she might be forced to admit to her parents what happened in DC, and she never planned to tell anyone that unpleasant story.

Bunking at Logan's place would give her time to figure out how to start moving forward again. She could use the time to look for a flexible job, a new place to stay, and a roommate. Easy.

The only difficult part of the scenario would be resisting the mouthwatering Logan McCabe. Or she could embrace her impulsive nature and follow her sister's intriguing suggestion and enjoy a steamy fling. Both sexy as sin and allergic to commitment, Logan epitomized perfect fling material.

For the first time since moving back to Silver Bay, Kat's chest swelled with a combination of anticipation and delight. She'd have all summer to get her fill of smoking hot sex that would heat her cheeks to think about fifty years from now. As a bonus, sex with Logan would be an excellent distraction from worrying about the bigger problems in life that she had no idea how to handle.

Decision made.

Next step: seduce Logan. Which would likely be as difficult as convincing him to take his next breath of air. After all, how hard could it be to strike up a game with the world's biggest player?

•••

"I heard you asked my daughter to live with you?"

"Not exactly," Logan said, wondering how the news of his offer could travel faster than the tricked-out sports car he'd leased for the summer. He'd arrived at Richard Bennett's spacious corner office at Bennett Industries less than an hour after his talk with Kat.

"I called to find out how Kat was doing this morning. She informed me that you asked her to move in."

Ignoring the accusation in Richard's tone, Logan shrugged. "She needs a place to stay. I have the space. I told her she could crash there if she wants. Not sure what she's decided."

Richard took a deep breath and stared him down, looking like an older, pissed-off version of Pax. Logan sat back in one of the deep leather chairs in front of Richard's dark wood desk. He stretched his legs out in front of him and adopted a disinterested expression. Logan had mastered the skill of playing things cool years ago, a skill he would need to convince Richard that he didn't give a shit if his daughter stayed with him or not.

Truth was he did give a shit. In fact, he hoped she turned him down. He'd always been damn attracted to her, but he didn't do long-term. He wouldn't ruin his friendship with Pax by messing around with his little sister. While he enjoyed flirting with Kat and seeing how fired up he could get her with an outrageous comment or two, he would never touch her, at least not the way he'd wanted to since the first time he saw her.

If she moved in with him, he would be taking a lot of cold showers this summer. He should have left her along the side of the road yesterday. Okay, he couldn't have done that, but he sure as hell didn't have to tell her she could live with him. But his sense of self-preservation had momentarily crumbled when he'd heard her say she didn't have the money to get a place of her own.

Richard pushed back from his desk, stood abruptly, and began pacing his office. "Something is going on with Katherine that she refuses to share with any of us." Frustration shook his words. "It has been almost a year since she walked away from her career in DC. We know something happened there to send her life into this perpetual holding pattern. Her mother thinks she may have broken up with some guy or maybe loved someone who didn't return the sentiment."

Grimacing, Richard stopped pacing and kneaded the back of his neck. Logan could practically hear tendons cracking under the assault. Totally understandable. Talking about your adult daughter's love life could suck the joy out of any man's day.

"Unfortunately," Richard continued, "Kat overheard me say I didn't plan to enable the destructive lifestyle she's settled into any longer. She can't keep floating through life without any goals."

Logan tapped the chair's armrest with the fingers of his right hand. That explained Kat's search for a place to stay. It didn't explain where Richard was going with this conversation. "Do you want me to take back my offer?"

Richard returned to his desk, sank into his chair, and exhaled a frustrated sigh. "She's an adult. I'm not going to pretend I have any power over where she sleeps. With that said ... " He leaned forward in his chair and locked a steely-eyed gaze on Logan. "Katherine is fragile right now. The last thing she needs is to become romantically involved with a man who's only in the country for a few months. I'm afraid another heartbreak would do irreparable damage."

Ah, shit. Logan clenched his jaw as a feeling of dread landed heavy in his gut. So now if he didn't keep his hands off of Kat, he would piss off both Pax and Richard, as well as hurt Kat while she was struggling to get her feet under her again.

"I hope you understand my concern," Richard said. "And I hope I can trust you."

"I won't do anything to hurt her," Logan said, for once grateful for Kat's open animosity toward him. She'd do all the heavy lifting in making sure he kept his word. After all, the little tiger would likely bite off his hand if he ever tried to touch her.

FOUR

RELAXING on a kitchen barstool, Kat took a sip of her crisp Pinot Grigio and congratulated herself on a successful day. In less than twelve hours' time, she'd cleared her stuff out of her parents' house, moved into Logan's spare room, taken Mrs. Dobolek to a doctor's appointment in Sheboygan, and filled the cottage with a plethora of tasty groceries.

She'd even managed to swing by Danny's garage to make an appointment to fix Bruno's air conditioner tomorrow. Poor Mrs. D. had looked miserable on the blazingly hot drive to her orthopedic surgeon. Kat couldn't keep chauffeuring the elderly in a heatstroke-inducing car.

And it seemed another senior citizen was joining her crew. Mrs. D. had asked her to take one of her friends, Harry Wilkinson, to his chiropractor's appointment in Green Bay tomorrow. Kat couldn't make the poor old guy sit in a pool of his own sweat for the hour-long drive. It figured the biggest heat wave in years would hit the same week her car's air conditioner crapped out.

She looked up at the sound of the front-door knob rattling, then smirked at the muttered oath that quickly followed. She rolled her eyes and strolled toward the door. About halfway there she heard a heavy thud—most likely a bulky shoulder—slam against the door. "Chill out. I'm coming."

"Kat, the bloody door is stuck."

She flipped the bolt, opened the door, and shot Logan a you're-an-idiot look. "It's not stuck. It's locked. And you better get used to it because I'm not living in a cottage where anyone can come and go on whim."

"So you're moving in?"

"Already have." She smiled. "I like to move fast."

He gulped. He actually gulped, and he looked nervous. She cocked her head and studied him closely. His blue eyes flitted around the cottage as he tapped his fingers against his leg.

"I've never seen you fidget before. Are you still okay with me living here?"

"Of course. And I don't fidget." Logan towered over her as he moved into the kitchen and sniffed. "Are you cooking?" He looked her way with an eyebrow raised.

"Yep. Glazed salmon with a smoky artichoke salsa."

"Huh. I didn't figure you as domestic."

"Everyone has to eat." She shrugged. "Might as well make the food taste good while you're at it. Would you like a glass of white?"

"Sure. I could use one after today."

Kat poured a glass of wine for Logan and

gestured to one of the barstools stationed around the kitchen island. "Have a seat and tell me about it."

Logan lowered himself onto a stool and accepted the glass she offered him with a grateful smile. "Before today, I'd only met with your mum to talk about the social outreach program. Today, I met with your dad. He can be very … " Logan paused and blew out a long breath. "Challenging."

"Sounds like Dad," Kat said, nodding her head dramatically.

"Both of your parents envision a program that creates solidarity in the community. They want local volunteers to perform the majority of the work, but they don't know what the volunteers should be doing or who they should be helping." Logan paused and took a drink of his wine. "I threw a dozen different ideas at your dad today, and he shot down every single one of them."

Kat thought for a moment. "How about building houses for the poor?"

"There's already a local charity doing that work. Your dad wants to be unique."

"Maybe you could do something for kids." Kat rummaged through the cabinets, gathering what she needed to chop the ingredients for the salsa. "Or people with disabilities."

"Both good causes, and both have heaps of charities or organizations already established to help them." Logan dipped his head and rubbed his fingertips against his forehead, a careless curve of hair nearly covering one of his crystal-blue eyes. "Your dad vetoed both. He wants to be unique."

"I sense a theme." Kat grinned and began chopping the artichoke hearts, tomatoes, and red onion and scraping them into a large glass bowl.

Logan snorted and took another drink of wine.

"What about helping the elderly?" she asked nonchalantly, well aware that there were many seniors in Silver Bay who could use a little extra help from their neighbors. "Your volunteers could assist them with everyday tasks they can no longer do themselves." She dumped the remaining ingredients into the salsa and gave everything in the bowl a few good turns with a wooden spoon. Stepping away, she checked the salmon in the oven.

"Is there a need for that?" he asked, his tone skeptical.

"You bet. There are people all over town you could help," she said, her back still to Logan. There. She'd planted the seed. He could decide whether or not to run with her suggestion without her admitting to her recent philanthropic activities.

Despite being outspoken at times, Kat didn't share her own personal information easily. The thought of telling Logan, or anyone, about helping Mrs. Dobolek and friends made her squirm.

She took a deep breath and turned around. Logan was leaning his elbows on the island and toying with the stem of the wineglass with one large hand. He looked so damned oversized sitting on the small stool she nearly rolled her eyes. While she could still ride in her niece's battery-powered Barbie car if she folded her body into it just right, Logan dwarfed normal-sized furniture.

The thought ticked her off.

Scowling, she flicked her hand toward his body. "You're ridiculously large."

Logan blinked. A beat later, a slow, devilish smile

curled his lips upward. "Thank you, darl, you've mentioned that before."

"And it's still not a compliment," she growled, surprised he recalled the conversation in Costa Rica when she'd grumbled about his overwhelming size.

Logan laughed—a deep, rumbling thing that turned her insides to liquid. "Ah, Kat, you really are a tiger."

She scooped up her glass and drained the rest of her wine, attempting to will her temper under control. If she planned to seduce this guy, she should probably be a little nicer.

Sure, she knew why he put her on edge, but she didn't like what it said about her, so she usually chose to ignore it. The truth was, being so physically pulled to a horndog like Logan didn't sit well with her, but no matter how hard she tried, she wasn't able to rein in her pulse-racing, body-tightening, lip-biting, pupil-dilating attraction to him.

But that no longer mattered. Claire's brilliant suggestion to have a short-term affair with him meant Kat didn't have to control her desire or fight her attraction any longer. Finally, the lust humming through her veins complemented rather than complicated her plans.

She licked her lips and tried not to grin. Now seemed like the perfect time to initiate her seduction plan. Considering Logan was her target, it shouldn't take much effort on her part.

She slipped on an oven mitt and pulled the glass dish holding the fish from the oven. "The salmon is ready, but I'm going to change before we eat. I spilled a little salsa on my top." She pointed to drop of tomato juice on her shirt.

"Righto," Logan said, standing from the barstool. "I'll set the table."

Kat hustled into her bedroom, kicked the door shut with her foot, and stripped the loose-fitting shirt over her head. A quick rifle through her closet revealed a complete lack of seduction-worthy clothes. She grunted in annoyance and searched through the closet again, hoping the slutty-clothes fairy had made a magical delivery without her noticing.

Damn. No such luck. There were no short skirts or plunging necklines in sight. Time to improvise.

The snug-fitting denim capris she already had on would be fine if she could find a lust-provoking top to pair with them. She glanced back to the closet and spotted a simple black tank top she used for layering under other shirts. A smile curved her lips. Bingo.

She slipped it from the hanger and held the thin, silky material in her hand and considered her options. Should she change into a bra designed to lift and shove her breasts to a position just below her chin, or should she go the more natural and more daring route?

Enjoying a surge of feminine power, Kat undid the front clasp on her bra, dropped it to the floor behind her, and slipped the form-fitting tank over her head. She quickly adjusted her unrestrained breasts to their full and upright position and turned to the mirror hung on the back of the door.

Her breasts weren't overly large, but they were full and perky as hell. Even without a bra, they were right where they needed to be to get a guy's attention. And if the rounded cleavage above the neckline didn't catch Logan's eye, the outline of her nipples under the tight black material should do the trick.

She removed the clip holding her hair in a ponytail and finger combed the waves into a sexy, tousled look. After a quick application of black mascara and shiny red lip gloss, she took a deep breath. One look and Logan would know exactly what she had in mind. She grinned in anticipation. Unless the big guy had an unlikely aversion to easy brunettes, the rest of her clothes would be tossed to the floor faster than she could say "g'day, mate."

•••

Logan placed the neatly folded napkin across the dinner plate and stepped back to admire his work. It'd been a lot of years since he'd set a table with such care and attention to detail.

When he was old enough, his mum had gotten him a job at a fancy country club just outside of Sydney that only the elite of Sydney's society could join. His mum worked there as a server, and he'd started out as part of the waitstaff, mainly clearing and setting tables. Eventually, he'd moved up to a server too, then a lifeguard, and eventually an instructor in the club's high-end fitness center.

The wealthy families had been kind and generous to him the first few years. The mums and their daughters had flirted with him, and the men had loved to hear about his latest victory on the rugby field. Even though he'd only been an employee, Logan had felt like he fit in there.

But it had all been an illusion. In the end, he'd learned the bloody truth. The rich would never truly

47

accept a kid who lived in a tiny house and rode a beat-up motorbike to work. Athleticism and charm could never replace a fancy education or family money.

It had been a valuable lesson. He'd learned what he had to offer a woman worked best in the short run. A woman might love having her panties charmed off her for a one-night stand. But when it came to her future, she would damn well want a bloke who could provide her with more than a wink and a smile.

"Are those napkins folded into the shape of the Sydney Opera House?"

Logan chuckled at the sound of surprise in Kat's voice behind him. "I'm good with my hands." He shot her a cocky look over his shoulder and then did a double take.

Holy shit.

Kat had transformed from tiger to sex kitten. She tipped her head to the side and ran a hand through her long dark hair. It was framing her face in an I-just-got-laid kind of style. Her lips looked wet and full, like they would if they'd been pashing for the last hour rather than talking about work. The black top hugged her slender frame tightly and spilled her firm breasts over the top into a tempting display.

"What a coincidence," she said, walking to stand directly in front of him. "I am too," she purred, tip-toeing her fingers up his chest.

"Good to know," Logan said, his voice thick. He gulped to clear his throat, stared at her hand on his chest, and tried not to look down her top. He failed miserably. And that's when he spotted the pert outline of her nipples under her painted-on shirt.

Shit. Damn. His body tightened and blood rushed south. What was she up to? He thought she would be the one to make sure their relationship never advanced. How the hell was he supposed to keep his hands off her if she kept putting hers on him?

"Let's eat before the fish gets cold." He moved into the kitchen and gratefully used the island as a barrier between them. Eyes down, he fumbled through plating the fish.

"Are you okay?"

"Me? Yip. I'm ace." He cringed at the unusual rush to his words and kept his eyes averted while he walked past her, set the plates on the table, and took a seat in one of the far chairs. "Smells great. I'm starving." He could feel her staring at him. Tension hummed through him.

Damn. He hated tension.

"You forgot the salsa." Kat retrieved the glass bowl from the kitchen and sauntered toward him. She stopped next to him, her sweet scent intoxicating him. Holding the bowl in one hand and a spoon in the other, she leaned over his right shoulder. Her breasts inches from his face, she tipped her head to look back at him, causing her hair to fall like a curtain, wrapping them in an intimate cocoon. Her lips curved into a sexy smile. "I like it on top," she murmured, paused a beat, and then poured a spoonful of salsa over the fish.

Logan jumped up, bolted to the opposite side of the table, and shoved a hand through his hair. "What the bloody hell are you doing?" he snapped.

Her blue eyes flashed with irritation. "If I have to explain it, then I must be doing it wrong."

49

He blew out a breath. "That depends. If you're trying to drive me out of my mind, then you're doing just fine."

"I'm not trying to drive you out of your mind. I'm trying to drive you into my bed. I want to have a no-strings, enjoy-the-moment fling. And you, Logan McCabe, are perfect fling material." She scanned his body and crossed her arms over her chest, effectively boosting her breasts even higher and further out of her top.

"Damn it, Kat. Can you please stop that?" He ground his teeth and turned his head to look blindly out the large window.

"What? Trying to seduce you?"

"No. Yes. Damn it." His voice boomed. "Just stop all of it. I can't sleep with you."

"Why the hell not?" she demanded.

"Because I promised your father I wouldn't touch you." Belated warning bells sounded in Logan's head as he watched Kat's face register simultaneous shock, outrage, and fury.

"You did what?" she roared.

Logan lifted his hands in a palms-out gesture. "Calm down. It's not a big deal. He's worried about you, that's all. Besides, even if I hadn't promised your dad, Pax would kill me if I ever touched you."

Kat eyed him for a long, hard ten seconds. An instant later, she sighed and all the tension slipped from her body. "Phew. That's a relief. I thought you were going to tell me you aren't attracted to me."

"What?" Logan asked, eyes wide and incredulous. "Are you crazy? You're gorgeous, smart, funny, tough as nails, and sexy as hell." He blew out a breath and shook his head. "I couldn't be more attracted to you."

"You keep that up and you're going to make me blush," she said with a chuckle. "Are you sure you're not afraid that you could become too attached to me if we had a fling? I'd hate to break your heart." She shot him a cheeky smile.

The tension eased from his body. Kat wasn't pissed at him after all, just relieved to know his reasons for not sleeping with her had everything to do with her dad and Pax and nothing to do with her.

"No worries, darl. My heart doesn't do broken. Which means in most cases, you're right, I am perfect fling material."

"So my dad and brother are the only reason you don't want to have a hot, steamy affair while you're in Silver Bay?"

"Absolutely." He nodded, thrilled she was taking this so well.

"Thanks for being honest, Logan. That's really helpful to know." She sat down at the table and gestured for him to do the same. "We should eat before the food gets any colder."

Exhaling a sigh of relief, he took his seat again, grabbed a piece of bread from the basket on the table, and slathered on some butter. "Thanks heaps for making dinner. Living with someone who can cook is a major bonus. I have a good feeling about the next few months," he said and popped the piece of bread into his mouth.

"I'm confident a lot of things are going to feel really, really good during the next few months." Kat locked her smoldering gaze on him as she gently swirled the wine in her glass.

The warning bells fired back up in his head.

"But, your father—"

"I'm a grown woman, Logan," Kat interrupted. "I have no intention of letting the unrealistic and chauvinistic wishes of my father or brother eff up my sex life." Her determined gaze burned into him "You just admitted those two idiots are the only reason we're not having hot, crazy sex right now. That's a total bullshit reason to forgo the fling we both want to have." She leaned forward and arched her back, drawing his wayward gaze back to her cleavage. "I'll do what it takes to convince you I'm right."

Logan cursed under his breath, tore his gaze from her chest, and glanced toward the front door. While tempting, he knew running from the house would only be a temporary solution. Why the bloody hell had he been stupid enough to crash with a tiger?

FIVE

BRIGHT rays of morning sunshine slipped through the blinds on Kat's windows, filling the room with cheerful warmth and the dazzling promise of a new day. She stretched her arms over her head and grinned. She hadn't slept so deeply or so peacefully in almost a year.

Man, she felt great. Watching Logan squirm through dinner last night was the most fun she'd had in ages.

When she first heard about the idiotic deal he'd made with her dad, she considered throttling him. Thankfully for him, just before she relocated his boys with her knee, she realized how much fun she could have persuading him to break the stupid promise instead.

For as long as she could remember, probably dating back to the arrival of her breasts, boys had hit on her. Not that she was all that, but she was reasonably attractive, and her body was firm where it should be firm and soft where it should be soft. In her experience, that was more than enough to draw attention from the opposite sex.

But until last night, she'd never realized the exhilaration of being the sexual aggressor in a situation. For the first time since that crappy night in DC, she felt strong and in control, like she wasn't a goddamn wuss afraid of the frickin' boogeyman.

Of course, it helped a ton knowing Logan wanted her. No way could she ever come on to a guy that strongly if he wasn't one hundred percent interested. Now that she knew Pax and her dad were the only things stopping Logan from sleeping with her, she felt confident in tempting him.

Pumped to start the day, Kat hopped out of bed, slipped on a sporty tan skirt and her favorite top— an über-soft, formfitting red T-shirt that suggested SAVE WATER DRINK BEER. One trip to the bathroom and two flip-flops later, and she was ready to go.

She slung her large tote over her shoulder, sauntered out of her room, and spotted Logan standing in the kitchen, rushing through a bowl of cereal. The poor guy hadn't even taken time to sit down. If his hurried breakfast wasn't a big enough clue, the look of panic that crossed his face the moment he saw her made it perfectly clear he'd hoped to avoid her.

"Relax, big guy." She patted his shoulder as she walked by. "I've got a busy day. No time for seduction, I'm afraid." She snagged an apple from the fridge, dropped it into her tote, and began rummaging through the large bag in her daily key-hunt routine.

"Nice shirt."

She looked up to find Logan's gaze locked on her chest, a sexy smile playing around his lips.

"What can I say? I'm a conservationist." She shrugged and continued digging blindly for her keys.

"I'm pretty sure that's not the message it's trying to send," Logan said dryly.

She waved away his comment. "We can argue semantics later. Right now, I've gotta find my keys. I swear my purse has a portal to another dimension hidden in there somewhere." She started dumping the contents, scattering a hairbrush, multiple lip glosses, a pair of dangly earrings, her phone, an e-reader, and a can of tuna across the countertop. "One time I put a set of dentures in there and couldn't find them again for three days. No way were they in there the whole time. They must have crossed into another dimension. Obviously, it's the only explanation."

"Obviously," Logan agreed, a look of amusement quirking one eyebrow north. "Wait. Why did you have fake teeth in your purse? And what's the tuna for?"

"Found them!" Kat pulled her yin-yang keychain from the oversized bag and thrust the keys dramatically into the air while she strutted out a few victorious dance moves.

Logan chuckled and poured a glass of orange juice. "This is a big deal for you."

"My day is packed. I'd hate to start off behind schedule. That reminds me: I have you penciled in for six tonight. Does that time work for you or is later better?"

Juice glass halfway to his mouth, he froze and shifted his gaze to her, panic etched in his features.

"I thought you didn't have time for seduction today?"

"Yes, today I'm busy. But my night is free." She waggled her eyebrows at him.

A strangled sound came from his throat.

She laughed and rolled her eyes at the insane level of tension gripping his body. For being such a carefree guy, he sure looked ready to implode. "Don't get your panties in a bunch. I bought a couple of steaks yesterday. I thought you could be a good mate and throw them on the barbie, ay." She threw in an Australian accent for fun.

"Now that's something I can agree to." He tipped his glass to her in a mock salute, then drained the juice in one gulp. "But I've got a late meeting this afternoon. I won't be home by six. Is seven too late for dinner?"

"Seven is perfect." On her way to the front door, Kat trailed her hand along Logan's very fine butt as she walked past him. "See you then, big guy," she murmured, channeling her best inner vixen.

She hustled out the door before he had time to change his mind about dinner, and jumped into her car. She hadn't been joking—she really did have a busy day. She needed to get Bruno's air conditioner checked, get a job, take an old dude to his doctor's appointment in Green Bay, hit the grocery store with Mrs. D., and squeeze in time to slut-up her wardrobe. Seriously. That was a lot of stuff for one day.

Twenty minutes later, Kat dropped her car at Danny's shop and headed to Hannah's café on foot while she munched on her apple. It was still early, so the temperature hadn't rocketed past tolerable yet, and as a bonus, a nice breeze was blowing off the lake. With any luck, today wouldn't reach the same hotter-than-hell level of the past few days.

A few blocks later, she tossed the core of her apple into the trash, crossed Main Street, and tugged open the glass door leading into Fresh.

Only two blocks from the lake's shore, her sister's coffee shop held a piece of prime real estate directly on the town's much-loved downtown square. Stepping into the eclectic room, Kat sucked in a deep breath. The smell of rich coffee and warm pastries instantly convinced her she needed more to start her day than an apple.

Walking toward the counter, Kat scanned the shop. Hannah had a special touch when it came to design, and she'd done a great job making Fresh a welcoming oasis. The walls were original brick, the artwork colorful, the tables and chairs artfully mismatched, and the atmosphere buzzing with caffeine-induced happy chatter.

She recognized about half the people there. The ones she didn't know were likely tourists in town to enjoy the lake on the hottest days of July. Like many lakeside towns, Silver Bay's numbers went up in the summer and dropped off with the arrival of winter temperatures in late fall. When the weather went south so did the tourists.

Still three back in line, Kat spotted Hannah rushing out of the back room carrying a tray of fruit tarts in one hand, two bottles of flavored syrups balanced in the other, and a huge pack of napkins tucked under her arm.

At thirty, Hannah was two years older than Kat and third in line of the four Bennett kids. She shared

Kat's dark hair, light complexion, and wide smile. In contrast to Kat, however, Hannah reached medium height and with high enough heels could actually look tall. She was also way nicer to people—likely the unfortunate outcome of being a peace-making middle child in Kat's opinion.

"Hey, sis. Heard you need a hand, and I'm looking for a job."

Hannah glanced up and smiled. "If you can start now, you're hired. Justin called in sick today, and we're slammed."

"You're in luck. I'm free for a few hours." Kat circled behind the counter, slipped a teal apron around her neck, pulled her hair back into a messy knot, and scrubbed her hands before moving to the register. "But I've got to head out by eleven."

"What's at eleven?" Hannah asked, efficiently filling a large cup with coffee.

"Really hot date with an older man." At least it would be if Danny didn't get her air conditioner fixed by then.

Hannah quirked an eyebrow in interest but didn't comment until after they'd handled the worst of the morning rush a few hours later. "Okay, it's rarely empty here, but it should be slower now until lunch. You mentioned a hot date. I want details."

"I'm not sure you could handle hearing *those* details." Kat winked and clicked her tongue at her sister. "I wouldn't want to make you blush." Which was a total lie, of course. Kat loved teasing Hannah.

"Please." Hannah rolled her eyes. "I'm older than you."

"Age doesn't equal experience, honey. When's the last time you got laid?"

"Shh!" Hannah looked around to see if anyone was listening to their conversation. "My customers don't want to hear about my sex life or lack thereof."

"Hannah, there are four, count them, four tables with single men at them."

"So? A lot of men like coffee."

"True, but each of those guys is sitting in a chair facing the counter rather than looking out over the square."

"That doesn't mean—"

"And they all keep glancing up to watch you work when you're not looking."

"Really?" Hannah asked, her voice rising to a squeak as she shot a nervous glance toward the front of the café.

"Yup." Kat tipped her head in the direction of one poor dude sitting solo at a small table along the outside wall. "Look at Mike Saunders. You remember him, right? He was in Pax's class. The guy hasn't turned a single page in that mammoth novel stationed in front of him. How often does he lug that thing in here anyway?"

A second after Hannah shifted her eyes to Mike, he looked up, caught her staring, and smiled like he'd just won the frickin' lottery.

Kat shook her head. "That's just sad. I've never seen a guy so excited over eye contact. Talk about low-hanging fruit. You should totally go out with him."

"I'm too busy to date a bunch of guys right now. Fresh is my priority."

"I said to date one of them, not all of them at once."

"I. Am. Not. Dating. Anyone."

"All right. Fine. But, seriously, Hannah, you've gotta throw these guys a bone. At least start wearing short skirts instead of jeans every day."

"I can't wear short skirts to work." Hannah looked as if Kat had suggested she serve coffee topless on Tuesdays. "It would be a peep show every time I bent over to wipe down a table."

"Exactly." Kat poured herself a cup of coffee and snatched a yogurt parfait from the chilled case. "Mind if have a snack?"

"Please do. You're making my eyelid twitch." Hannah pressed her fingertips to her closed eye. "If your mouth is full, I won't have to hear any more of your crazy ideas."

"You love me."

Hannah sighed. "I do, but you don't make it easy." She grabbed a towel and began wiping off two recently vacated tables. "So is your hot date with Logan?"

"Nope." Kat grinned. "But I am going to live with him for the summer."

"Really?" Hannah asked, clearing away empty cups from a high-top table in the corner. "Claire told me about your conversation yesterday. I assume you took her advice and refused to move out."

Kat's grin widened. "Actually, I've decided to take all of Claire's advice regarding Mr. McCabe."

Hannah spun around to face her, her hazel eyes wide. "You mean a wild, passionate fling?"

"That's the plan."

"You sure that's a good idea? Guys can cause a lot of problems."

"That's the beauty of the whole thing." Kat smirked. "He's in the country for less than three months. How much trouble can he cause in that amount of time?"

"Famous last words," Hannah mumbled, skepticism etched on her delicate features. "Have you guys mingled limbs yet?"

Kat cocked her head to the side. "Huh?"

"You know ... " Hannah looked around to make sure no one was close enough to hear their conversation. "Have you parallel parked? Played a game of horizontal Tetris? Churned the butter?"

"Sex," Kat said dryly. "The word you are looking for is sex. And, no, we haven't had sex yet. But we will soon. No way can he hold out much longer."

"Hold out? He turned you down?" Hannah asked, her tone a flattering combination of outrage and shock.

"Well, yeah, sorta." Kat shrugged. "But he wasn't very convincing. I'll change his mind."

"And if you don't?"

"Please. I'm crashing with a guy who's easier to do than a ten-piece jigsaw puzzle." Kat leaned into the pastry counter and picked out two plump chocolate chip cookies. She slipped them into a pastry bag and dropped the bag into her tote. "Mind if I take a couple cookies with me?"

"Are you planning to use chocolate chip cookies to bribe Logan?"

"Nah. These are for my hot date with Harry."

"Wait. Who's Harry?" Hannah asked, wrinkling her nose in confusion.

"The older guy I mentioned earlier."

"What about Logan? Doesn't he get a cookie?"

"Nope." Kat winked at her sis. "He hasn't earned a cookie yet."

•••

Two hours before her dinner date with her hunky roommate, Kat pulled her sweatbox car to a slow, tired stop in front of the cottage. She blew out a sigh of relief, peeled her sweaty thighs from the leather seat, and stepped from the car. Unfortunately, Danny had to order a part to fix her air conditioner that wouldn't arrive until Monday. Which meant she had another four days of transporting seniors in a sauna. Super.

Sauntering toward the house and carrying two shopping bags full of new and hopefully lust-inspiring clothes, Kat tilted her head from side to side, enjoying the snap, crackle, and pop of her neck. After listening to Harry rave about his chiropractor's magical hands on the drive home from Green Bay, her own neck and back felt like they had more knots in them than the cottage's pine floors.

She needed to cool down and unwind before Logan returned. Since a relaxing dip in Lake Michigan would accomplish both, Kat beelined to her room and yanked a teeny black bikini from the shopping bag. Rather than taking time to dig for scissors in the kitchen, she strong-armed the tags off, kicked off her sticky clothes, and wiggled into the suit.

After a few minutes of adjusting the top—which looked more like two eye-patches laced together by a shoestring—she had all the essentials behind fabric. Glancing at the mirror, she swallowed down a moment of doubt at the suit's lack of coverage. Unlike every other bikini she owned, this one didn't hug her body, providing support and assistance in the process. Nope. This frickin' suit was draped across her, held loosely in place by a few flimsy strings and a whole lot of luck.

Kat grabbed a towel, crossed through the back porch, and zipped down the stairs toward the lake. She dropped her towel on the back of an Adirondack chair and strode to the water, her breasts jiggling obnoxiously. While they weren't huge, she'd been told that—much like herself—her breasts were a handful, and that had always been just fine by her. Now she actually felt grateful they weren't any bigger. Lord knows anything larger would likely bounce right out of this barely there top.

She waded into the lake and sighed in bliss as the water lapped at her over-heated skin. As a strong wind whipped her hair around her face and shoulders, she worked through the breaking waves until she reached the shoulder-deep water beyond. She smoothed her uncontrolled hair from her face and slipped under the water.

Cool relief enveloped her, relaxed her, and doused the remaining flames of the ninety-degree day. She stayed underwater until her air supply gave out, enjoying the respite.

Her family was right. She had needed a jumpstart to get her life moving forward again. And crashing with Logan had definitely moved her life in a good direction. Sure, she didn't have a career and still feared being alone at night, but at least she had more fun things to think about now—like seducing a sexy Aussie.

She'd worry about the other crap later.

The low hum of a powerful engine drew her gaze

toward the lane leading from the highway. She watched Logan's red car draw closer, then slip from view behind the cottage. A few minutes later, he strolled around the side of the house, heading toward the lake. He plunked down on the chair holding her towel and cocked his head to the side, staring directly at her.

"Come on in," Kat yelled. "The water's great."

A boyish smile lit his face. "Says the Big Bad Wolf."

"I promise not to bite." Kat paused. "Unless you want me to."

Logan tipped his head back and laughed. "You sound like you're kidding, but I'm half-afraid you're not."

Kat chuckled and began moving toward the shore. "Fine. I'll come out if you're too chicken to join me." When she reached chest-deep water, she paused. She could tell the knot of her suit top had slipped a little. If she didn't want to flash Logan, she probably should tighten it before going any farther. Reaching behind her, she pulled the string loose and attempted to retie it.

And that was the moment the powers-that-be decided to have some fun. A powerful wave slammed into her back. She let out a strangled yelp, threw her hands in front of her in a useless effort to counterbalance, and tumbled face first into the lake.

A second after going under, she found her footing on the sandy bottom and popped her head out of the water. She gasped in a breath, stood to her full height, and slicked her long hair away from her face. She opened her eyes and looked at Logan, expecting to see him chuckling after watching her belly flop into the water.

Instead, his eyes were hot, dark, and transfixed on her. Well, on her chest to be more specific. She reached up to adjust her top, but there was no top to adjust.

Holy hell. She sucked in a horrified breath. Her breasts were bare. Completely frickin' bare! She shot a horrified look at the beach and spotted two pieces of minuscule triangular black fabric sprawled in the sand. The damn wave had lifted the top of her flimsy suit over her head and carried it to shore.

She fisted her hands, fighting back the nearly overwhelming desire to cover herself. She wanted this. Well, obviously, not this exact situation, but she did want Logan to look at her the way he was right now. Even though she hadn't planned on using nudity to get through his defenses, it seemed to be working pretty well for her. Might as well go with it.

She tipped her chin up and pinned him with her gaze as she slowly strolled toward the beach. She felt her nipples harden as both the summer breeze and Logan's gaze caressed her body. She scooped her top out of the sand. Tension thickened the humid air and intensified the desire building under her tiny bikini bottom.

"If you keep looking at me like that, big guy, we might not have time to grill our steaks." She stretched her arms up and wrung water from her hair, proud of her casual tone. Maybe he would be more likely to break the idiotic promise to her dad if he thought she walked around naked in front of guys all the time.

"Can't stop," he growled, his voice low and rough.

She felt a slow grin lift the corners of her mouth. "Good." She stepped between his thighs and stopped only when her own legs bumped into the front of his chair. Then she slowly leaned forward and reached her arms around his neck. The heat of his breath grazed her nipples. Her core melted, and every cell in her body came alive.

"Kat ... " Her name sounded like a warning on his lips. But she also heard an unmistakable craving in his tone.

"Sorry, darl," she said in a husky voice. "You're leaning on my towel." She lifted her towel from the back of his chair, wrapped it around her shoulders, and took a small step back.

Logan squeezed his eyes closed, fisted his hands on the chair's armrests, and drew in a shaky breath.

She slowly trailed the back of her index finger down his cheek and across his full bottom lip. "Why fight the attraction between us? We're both single, and neither of us want a commitment. Let's enjoy the summer together."

Logan opened his eyes and sighed. "I made a promise."

"A stupid-ass promise," she snapped.

"I promised not to hurt you." Logan abruptly stood up, stepped away from her, and shoved a hand through his hair. "My relationships have a history of ending badly. If we sleep together ... " He paused, shaking his head slowly. "I'm not sure I can keep that promise."

Open-mouthed, Kat watched him stride away from her. She'd always thought he was nothing more than a gorgeous, fun-loving guy, but he'd just walked away from an easy score. If nudity couldn't get him to break his promise, what the hell would?

She blew out a sigh and slumped into the chair. Just her frickin' luck. She picked a guy to seduce who hid a strong moral character behind a devil-may-care smile. Sure, she could try to find a different guy to have a casual affair with, but that idea left her feeling flat, and unmistakably disappointed.

She ground her teeth together. Damn Logan. She'd never even slept with him, yet it somehow felt like the jerk had ruined her for other men.

Ugh. Royally ticked at the thought, Kat jumped to her feet and stormed toward the house. No way would she quit so easily. She simply needed to rethink her approach. Her advances had been as direct as a smack upside the head. Logan might lower his guard and forget about that stupid promise to her dad if she employed a smidgen of subtlety.

Time for Plan B.

SIX

IT took two hours and multiple beers for Logan's blood to cool after the heated scene with Kat on the beach. It should have helped that she'd put on an unprovocative pair of shorts and loose-fitting tee for dinner, but it didn't. At least she hadn't brought up sex since she stormed into the house after her swim.

He liked Kat's family, and he liked her. He didn't want to hurt any of them. He needed to keep his word and keep his hands to himself. But he could only take so much. With Kat leaning over him—her perfect breasts wet and only inches from his mouth—he'd been so damn hard it hurt. If she hadn't covered up when she did, he would have caved and taken her right there on the sand.

"Why the scowl, big guy?"

"I don't scowl."

After a dinner of grilled steaks, asparagus, and something she called smashed potatoes, they'd moved to the screened-in porch with a beer in hand to enjoy the cool breeze blowing off the lake. Kat had dropped to the couch, kicked her feet onto the table in front of her, and stared toward the lake, seemingly lost in thought. Apparently, she'd switched to staring at him.

"Oh, I totally saw a scowl. You should be careful. Those things will wrinkle you up worse than a raisin under a sunlamp. I like to keep my life as free of stress as possible." She sipped her beer. "Maybe you should try yoga or something."

"I don't need yoga," he grumbled. If he could find a decent place to work out, he would be able to burn off some tension, but the nearest gym was small, outdated, and over thirty minutes away.

"Then you need to get laid." She winked and clicked her tongue. "That would definitely turn your frown upside down."

Logan grunted, dropped his head back, closed his eyes, and rubbed his temples where he could feel a mother of a headache forming. He'd been trying not to think about Kat, her fantastic body, or getting laid since she moved in with him. But the more he tried not to think about it, the more he couldn't get it out of his head. Her bringing it up every five seconds didn't help.

Besides, she was right; he really did need to get laid. Preferably with Kat and preferably soon. But Richard said she was going through a tough time. If he used her for sex, he'd feel like shit afterwards. And feeling like shit stressed him out, and damn it, he hated stress. Then again, not sleeping with Kat also stressed him out. He couldn't win.

How the hell had his life gotten stuck spinning helplessly in a circle of stressful shit?

"You're scowling again."

He ground his teeth and rubbed his temples harder. He could feel the lines of tension etched in his face, so he didn't bother to deny it. Keeping his hands off Kat while they lived together would probably age him ten years. Hell, he'd consider himself lucky if a few wrinkles were the worst thing that happened to him this summer.

He'd only made the mistake of giving his heart to a woman once, when he was young and stupid. After that, he'd adopted the carefree attitude that worked so well for him. The only time things ever got mucked up was when someone tried to get serious. But Kat didn't want serious, so why was she twisting him into knots?

He took a deep breath to relax his features and lifted his head from the back of the couch to look at her again. She sat cross-legged, beaming a Cheshire-cat smile at him. She didn't fool him. Her wide smile might say charming and innocent, but the spark of mischief lighting her blue-gray eyes said she knew the effect she had on him.

"You enjoy torturing me."

Kat tipped her head back and laughed. And damn if it wasn't the sexiest thing he'd ever heard. The sultry, rich tones of her laughter oddly soothed and aroused him at the same time.

Christ, he was a fucking mess.

"I'm honestly not trying to tease, torment, or torture you. Well … not right now at least. Sorry if crashing together has made your life difficult. Can I do anything to make it easier?"

"Keeping your clothes on would help," he grumbled.

Kat's eyebrows shot up.

"I mean it, no more nudity. And you need to find a new bather for swimming, one with enough fabric to cover"—he gestured toward her body—"everything."

"Fine. Whatever. No nudity." She took another sip of her beer. Then, beer bottle still in hand, she pointed at him with her index finger. "But you really need to work on being less of a fun sponge."

"Huh?"

"You kinda suck the fun out of everything. You should loosen up, relax a little bit."

"What the hell are you talking about?" he snapped, grabbing his beer from the table with more force than necessary. "I'm a carefree, fun-loving guy." He ground the words out between clenched teeth.

Kat cocked her head to the side. "Most guys would jump at the chance of no-strings sex, and you just made me promise to keep my clothes on for the summer. Even though your reason for saying no is bullshit, you're still sticking to it. I hate to break it to you, Logan, but that makes you sound kinda mature and responsible, not carefree and fun-loving."

"Holy shit. I've turned into Pax." He dropped his head back again in misery. "I'm too bloody serious and more concerned about doing what's right than having a good time." He beat the back of his head against the hard cushion a few extra times as the depressing realization landed with a heavy thud in his gut. "I'm not sure if I should feel proud or disgusted."

"Don't sweat it. My brother is a great guy. And now that he's with Sage, they're having a lot of fun together. Besides, we all have to grow up sometime."

He lifted his head to study her. "Have you?" he asked hopefully.

"Hell no. I'm still lots of fun." Kat shot him a cocky smile, then picked up her phone seconds after it pinged with an incoming text. As she read the message, her smile slid away. "Frick," she mumbled under her breath and tossed her phone onto the cushion beside her.

"Problem?"

"The part for Bruno's air conditioner won't be in until Monday, and now I have somewhere to go Sunday. Since they're still predicting temperatures in the nineties the trip is going to suck. Seriously, when is this heat wave going to end?"

"You can take my car."

"For real?" Kat asked, eyes wide. "Your car is sweet. You'd let me drive it?"

"Sure. It's a short-term lease. I wanted a fun car since I'm such a fun guy," he added dryly.

Her pretty face fell. "Shoot. I forgot. It's a manual. I never learned how to drive a stick."

For some inexplicable reason, her melancholy tone and dejected expression made him want to do anything he could to make her happy. "I don't have any plans this weekend. I can teach you on Saturday."

"You will?" Kat clapped her hands in excitement. "I tried to learn when I was younger but couldn't figure it out. Now Dad refuses to let me try again with his car."

"Why not?"

She dismissed his question with a causal wave. "He's overly cautious. I'm a good driver, no matter what my family thinks."

"Am I going to regret this?" Logan asked pointlessly since he was already regretting it.

"Probably." She shrugged. "Apparently, I grind the gears a lot."

He cringed and rubbed the back of his neck. "I don't think a dropped transmission is covered in my insurance policy."

"Bummer." Kat hopped to her feet with a grin. "Too bad you're a man of your word. You're stuck with me now. I'm off to bed. Night, Logan." Kat gave him a saucy little wave and sauntered into the house.

"Goodnight, darl," Logan murmured, acutely aware of how empty the porch felt without her.

Whenever possible, she'd avoided him in Costa Rica. But here, in only a few days' time, he'd grown used to having her around. Though a tiny little thing, Kat could fill any room she walked into with presence alone. Yeah, she loved to torment him, but he loved her wit and smart-ass comments. She kept him guessing and kept him sharp—a refreshing change from the predictable women he usually hooked up with. He would miss her when he left.

Unease curled through him at the thought. He needed to be careful and keep his attraction to Kat from growing into anything serious. If he didn't, he could end up with a lot more to regret than a few wrinkles and a ruined transmission.

•••

Three days later, Logan yawned and leaned back against the kitchen counter. Today was driving lesson day, and he and Kat had gotten up early to hit the road while most people were still in bed. He hadn't seen her yet, but he heard her singing "Born to be Wild" while she got ready in the bathroom. It didn't bode well.

When her rendition ended, the bathroom door swung upon, and she strutted out in a black dress so short and tight his pulse kicked up a beat.

"What are you wearing?"

"This is my kick-ass driving outfit. Pretty awesome, right?"

"You look like you're in a motorcycle gang."

"Exactly. If I'm going to be flying around town in that hot little car of yours, I want to make sure I send the right message."

"Darl, 'bad girl' is the only message you're sending in those clothes."

"Sweet! Which reminds me. If any guys check me out while we're in the car, you need to duck down. That whole good-boy, Mister-Moral image you're sporting would totally ruin my street cred."

"You don't have any street cred," Logan pointed out dryly.

"I will after today. Now let's get to it." Kat grabbed his arm and dragged him out of the house.

He shook his head. "Whenever you say something outrageous—which is often—I am pretty sure you're kidding. But honest to God, I'm not positive."

Kat grinned from ear to ear. "It's part of my charm."

Logan laughed and slid into the passenger seat. "So, are you kidding?"

"Sometimes I am. Sometimes I'm serious. Usually, it's a bit of both." Kat climbed in behind the wheel.

"You were kidding about me hiding so you could pick up another guy in my car, right?"

"Nope." She shook her head. "That one I'm serious about."

Logan snorted. "Sorry, darl, no way in hell that's happening."

"You're jealous."

"I'm not jealous." Just because his chest burned at the thought of another guy hitting on Kat, didn't make him jealous.

"Don't sweat it. It's kinda cute." She winked. "Okay. How do I make this bad boy go vroom?"

After listening intently to his directions, Kat pushed in the clutch, shifted the car into first, eased up on the clutch, and applied the gas exactly as he'd instructed.

The car bucked twice and died.

Three more attempts, three similar results.

Kat's grip tightened on the wheel as she dropped her head back against the seat. "This is just like last time. I did precisely what I was supposed to do— four times—and it didn't work. Are you sure you didn't forget some crucial piece of information, like an incantation to chant when lifting the clutch?"

"No magic required, I promise." Logan chuckled as he rubbed the back of his neck, trying to think of a way to explain it to her. "You've got to feel the car. Really hear the engine and instinctively know what to do. Why don't you try letting up on the clutch slowly until you feel the car start to respond? Then just hold your foot there. Don't do anything else."

She looked skeptical but did as instructed. She slowly lifted her foot off the clutch and stopped the moment she felt the car start to react. With her foot held in that position, the car didn't move forward or die. It sat alert, waiting for her command.

Kat grinned. "It's working! I can feel it. What next?"

"Slowly start to push on the gas until you feel a catch. That means you've found a balance. Then continue to evenly lift the clutch and lower the accelerator at the same time. Pay attention to the car, and you'll soon recognize what it needs without having to think about it."

Kat squared her shoulders and adjusted her grip. This time the car moved forward, slowly, hesitantly, as if concerned about the driver's abilities.

"You nailed it, darl."

Kat laughed, her features bright with excitement as she turned onto the road and shifted into second. "I told you I was a great driver," she said, jerking the car into third.

When she tried to shift into fourth Logan shuddered at the mangled sound of the gears grinding in resistance. Even though every newbie made that mistake a few times, it was still tough to hear.

"Whoopsie. Forgot to use the clutch."

"No worries. You're doing great."

She tossed him a relieved smile and continued on toward Silver Bay. It soon became clear what Kat lacked in skill, she made up for in exuberance. While some of her starts were bumpy and others made the engine roar, the expression of pure joy on her face never faded.

Twenty minutes later, she pulled to a jerky stop in front of Hannah's coffee shop and let her foot off the clutch, forgetting to put the car in neutral first. The car bucked once and died.

"A suitable ending to a dramatic trip, don't you think?" Kat asked, her words a rush of excitement. "I mean, seriously, I totally rocked it!" She slugged his shoulder and grinned wide. "Come on, big guy. I'll buy you brekkie for your trouble." She popped out of the car and belted out the chorus of "Born to be Wild."

He swallowed a groan while he watched her ass sway from side to side as she moved toward Fresh's front door. He wanted Kat when she wasn't trying to seduce him just as damn much as he did when she was laying it on thicker than a stripper at a buck's night. And it seemed the more he got to know her, the more he wanted her.

Sure, he'd been attracted to her at La Vida. She was a gorgeous woman with a killer body and cheeky attitude that kept him alert, active, interested. But he hadn't spent as much time with her in Costa Rica as he would've liked. While she'd willingly participated in any excursion, adventure, or volunteer work led by anyone else at La Vida, she'd steered clear of any activity when he'd been in charge or if the situation meant they'd be alone together.

Now that he was living with her, he realized she could be playful and sweet as well as sexy as hell, which turned out to be a damn attractive combination. He needed to find something he didn't like about this woman. Something really shitty that would get rid of the lust and—even more scary—the fondness he felt for her. Maybe she enjoyed making fun of poor kids whose worn-thin pants were always a few inches too short. Or maybe she even kicked puppies in her free time.

Kat had to have flaws. Everyone did. He just needed to find hers. How hard could that be?

SEVEN

"YOU picked a great spot for people watching." Kat set two cups of coffee and a plate-sized cinnamon roll on the table Logan had selected while she bought breakfast. He'd picked one of her favorite spots at the front of the shop. Nestled beside the front window, it looked out over Silver Bay's historic square. The table was meant to seat four, but Logan filled his side completely with six foot four inches of mouthwatering male muscle. From seventeen to seventy, every woman in the place had already checked him out.

"There weren't many spots to choose from," Logan said, seemingly unaware of the attention he drew. "I can't believe how busy this place is early on a Saturday morning."

"Fresh is always busy," Kat said, taking a seat across from him.

"How do you like working here?"

"Great! It's fun to chat with everyone; plus I get free coffee on the job." She slid a cup his way.

"Speaking of coffee, I didn't know how you liked yours so I asked for it black with room for milk."

"Perfect. Thanks, darl." With a grateful smile, Logan picked up the cup. "Think I'll just touch it up a bit."

Kat sipped her black coffee and stared at his broad shoulders and great butt as he walked to the station with creamers, milks, shakers full of coffee-related spices, and various types of sweetener packets. Like some hoity-toity chef preparing a culinary masterpiece, Logan worked at the station for a frickin' long time. Pouring, shaking, stirring, taste-testing, then pouring some more.

She laughed under her breath as one eager twenty-something redhead sidled up beside him, sneaking furtive glances his way approximately every five seconds. Logan, gotta love him, seemed clueless to the whole episode, his focus completely on his coffee. Not even glancing in Red's direction, he moved over to make room for her, but that was it. Eventually, the girl gave up and stomped back to her table with a pissed-off expression.

At long last, he headed back toward the table, dodging his muscular frame through the scattered tables in the cafe. The dude really was big. When she'd first met him, his size had bothered her. Thankfully, her unease around large men had faded a bit. Come to think of it, she hadn't worried much about being alone at night recently either. Of course, she hadn't actually been alone; she'd been with Logan. And she couldn't imagine ever feeling afraid with him around.

"You're such a coffee diva," she said as he sat down.

He cocked his head. "Coffee diva?"

"You spent more time doctoring up that drink than it takes me to make an entire meal." She shook her head in mock disappointment. "What did you put in there anyway?"

A grin tugged at the corner of his lips. "Milk, two packets of raw sugar, some of that powdered vanilla stuff, and just a bit of cinnamon. How do you drink yours?"

"Black. Like Mother Nature intended."

"Sounds boring." He took a sip. "This is great. Costa Rican, yeah?"

Surprised and a little impressed, Kat sat up straighter and eyed Logan. "Yeah. It's organic fair trade coffee sourced from a group of small farms not far from La Vida. Honestly, I'm shocked you can taste anything over all that crap you dumped in there. How did I live at La Vida for a month and not know this about you?"

He arched an eyebrow. "You either avoided or ignored me at La Vida. Usually both," he grumbled.

"True," she agreed with a cheeky grin. "You didn't seem worth the trouble then."

"And now?" he asked, his voice a low, sexy rumble.

"Now, I'm trying to convince you that I'm worth the trouble." Kat winked and clicked her tongue before turning her attention to the gooey concoction on the plate between them. "Dive in. These cinnamon rolls are huge, so I thought we could share." She forked up a bite and slipped the warm goodness into her mouth, moaning in pleasure. "Hannah is an amazing baker. It's one of the many reasons this place is so popular."

When Logan didn't respond, she looked up to find his gaze locked on her mouth. His posture was rigid, and his baby blues had a look so hot that her panties nearly caught fire.

Oh, yeah. He wanted her. Maybe even as much as she wanted him. She felt the urge to grab his shoulders and shake him until he agreed to break the foolish promise he'd made to her dad. But she'd learned her lesson. He hadn't responded to aggressive tactics, so she would try a more subtle approach this go around.

"How's work? Found a group of Silver Bay citizens to help yet, Superman?" She took another bite of the cinnamon roll, then used her tongue to lap up the frosting melted onto her fork. Okay, not exactly subtle, but at least she hadn't flashed him her boobs this time.

"Huh?" Logan grunted, gratifyingly distracted.

"Work. How's it going?"

"Oh. Good." He looked away and shook his head, hopefully trying and failing to clear away thoughts of her. "Actually, not good. I told your dad about your idea to help the elderly, but he's not sure there's a need. He said that families usually take care of that stuff."

Kat snorted and rolled her eyes. "Dad's sheltered and fairly clueless about some things. Trust me, there's a need. If you're free tomorrow, I can show you."

"Show me what?"

"What I'm talking about," Kat snapped, already wishing she'd kept her mouth shut.

For some crazy reason, she felt vulnerable offering to let Logan see how she'd been helping

Mrs. D and her friends.

So what if he found out how she spent her time? She wasn't ashamed of anything, but allowing Logan inside her private life when she'd shut everyone else out felt a little too personal. Which was laughable since the thought of having sex with him didn't seem too personal at all.

"Forget it. You would likely cramp my style."

"Too late." He scooped up a huge chunk of roll on his fork. "You offered and I accept." He popped the bite into his mouth and grinned like a smug SOB while he chewed the gargantuan piece of roll.

"Feeling really proud of yourself, big guy?" she asked, dropping her voice and narrowing her eyes.

Logan swallowed then took a sip of coffee. "Absolutely. You're a real larrikin. I'm sure you cause all kinds of interesting mischief during the day."

"Larrikin?" Kat bit back a grin. "What do you imagine I do during the day?"

"Bully children? Throw rocks at stray cats? I'm not sure." Logan shrugged. "I can't be the only one you torment."

Kat rolled her eyes so dramatically this time she almost made herself dizzy. "I'd never pick on kids or cats!"

"What about puppies?" Logan asked hopefully.

"Nope. I love animals."

"Fine." He slumped back in his chair.

She cocked her head to the side. "Would you *prefer* I be mean to animals and kids?"

"Auntie Kat!" Before Logan had time to answer, an adorable bundle of petite blond energy charged across the room and jumped into her lap.

Kat grunted on impact, then pulled her niece in

for a tight hug. "Hey, kiddo. What are you doing here?"

"Mom's at one of Ty's games so Aunt Hannah said I could stay here with her."

"How was your trip to Chicago?" Kat asked.

"Great! We saw dolphins! Not in the lake. But in a really big pool inside. I wanted to swim with them, but Mom said they didn't let anyone do that. She said there are places in Florida you can go to swim with them, and I really want to do it. I want to be a dolphin trainer when I grow up. Mom said I would be a maroon biogist."

"Marine biologist?" Kat asked with a grin when Grace paused to catch her breath.

"Yeah, that's it! Mom said I will have to take a lot of science classes. That's okay. I started science at school this year, and I'm really good at it. We looked at a strand of our own hair really close with a microscope. It was cool! Who's he?" Grace abruptly pointed at Logan.

"Grace, this is Logan McCabe. He's one of uncle Pax's friends." Kat lifted her gaze to Logan, who looked amused. "Logan, this is Grace, Claire's seven-year-old daughter. She likes to hang out at the coffee shop with Hannah when her mom is busy or at one of her brother's soccer matches."

"I hate soccer! It's sooooo boring," Grace moaned and flopped backwards against Kat as if even the thought of soccer drained away her will to go on.

"Nice to meet you, Grace." Logan extended his hand and a killer grin to Grace.

Her niece's eyes bulged. "Whoa. You sound different." Grace put her little hand into Logan's massive one.

He grinned wider, shaking her hand gently. "That's 'cause I'm an Aussie. That means I'm from Australia, the Land Down Under."

"Down under what?" Grace asked, her little brow wrinkled in confusion.

Though Logan's blue eyes lit with amusement, he didn't laugh at Grace's question, thank God. Grace could be sensitive to adults laughing at her. Whenever it happened, her darling little face would blush in embarrassment. Kat knew the grown-ups didn't intend to hurt her feelings; they simply found her inquisitive nature cute. But their laughter obviously made Grace feel foolish.

"That's a good question," Logan said, nodding his head in approval. "It's because my country is far down south, so on a map it looks like it sits under most other countries. You'd love it there since we have lots of dolphins. There's even an island where you can feed wild dolphins at sunset every night. It's ace. You should ask your uncle Pax to take you sometime."

"Cool!" Grace said, a big smile lighting her face. "I'll go text him right now! Uncle Pax is awesome. I just know he'll say yes!"

Kat shot Logan a bemused look when Grace bolted through the café toward the stairs to Hannah's apartment. "Pax is going to be pissed. I should be mad at you too for getting her hopes up, but knowing Pax he'll probably say yes."

"Too right." Logan laughed, looking mighty pleased with himself. "Pax will never be able to tell that little shelia no. He'll try to stall for a couple years, but he'll do it."

"I like your style, Logan McCabe," Kat said, picking up her coffee cup and extending it toward him in the air.

With a dull thunk, Logan tapped his cup against hers. "Back at ya."

"Thanks," Kat murmured as realization landed hard in her belly.

She liked Logan. And not just because he was sexy and oozed charm. She *really* liked him. The guy had offered her a place to stay and taught her to drive a stick shift with his gorgeous car. Not only did he make her laugh, their verbal sparring always energized and lightened her spirit. He treated Grace with kindness and a genuine respect that a lot of adults didn't extend to kids. And even though it pissed her off, he'd refused to sleep with her because his screwed-up morals said it was the right thing to do.

She had misjudged him. He was a hell of a lot more than the hot bod and carefree smile he presented. Kat couldn't help but wonder why Logan kept the best parts of himself hidden from the world.

•••

After lunch the next day, Kat slugged Logan on the shoulder and scooped up his keys from the kitchen counter. "Let's hit the road."

"Where are we headed?"

"You'll see." She smirked.

"Are we going to get arrested?" he asked, following her out of the cottage.

"Never know." She tossed the words over her shoulder, stopping next to the driver's door. "You need to quit being such a wuss. Life's no fun when you're too afraid to live it."

A bubble of hope swelled in her chest the second the words left her mouth. That sounded like something the old Kat would have said. Old Kat wasn't afraid of anything. God, she missed Old Kat. It felt good to think she might be able to get little pieces of herself back over time.

Logan laughed and opened the passenger door. "Okay, tiger, I'll follow your lead today."

"Sweet. Now get in the back."

Logan's brow dipped in confusion. "The back. Why can't I sit up front?"

"We're picking up a friend, and she gets to sit shotgun."

"What about you?"

"Oh, I'm driving, big guy."

Logan stood firmly planted outside the car. "Kat, I don't fit in the bloody backseat. Look at me." He gestured up and down his big body. "I'd have to lose a foot and fifty pounds to sit back there."

"Then it was kind of a ridiculous car choice for you to make, huh?" She tipped her head to the side and gave him a you-should-have-known-better look. "Now stop whining and climb in, or I'm leaving your arse behind." She slid behind the wheel, slammed the door, and turned the key. The car purred to life around her.

Grumbling a few obscenities, Logan eventually maneuvered himself into the cramped backseat. Aside from smacking his head against the roof and almost shutting his foot in the door, he fit just fine.

It usually took twenty minutes to get to Silver Bay from the cottage. Cutting that time to fifteen,

Kat rolled to a stop in front of Mrs. D.'s small brick house in the heart of town.

"Why the bloody hell did I have to sit back here *before* you picked up your friend?" Logan grumbled from the teeny backseat.

"Figured we should make sure you fit before we left the cottage." Kat stepped from the car. "Wait here. I'll go get her."

She hustled to the front door and tapped out a jaunty knock, wondering if she should feel guilty that tormenting Logan really brightened her day. *Nah.* Logan was a good sport, and if his back hurt from the bumpy ride in the toddler-sized backseat, she would offer him a massage to work out the kinks later.

Grinning at the thought, Kat stepped back when Mrs. D. swung the front door open. Next to her former piano teacher, Kat felt like an Amazonian warrior. Mrs. D. was tiny. Hell, her whole body probably weighed as much as Logan's left leg.

While the older lady always favored wearing pastels over neutrals, today she'd really embraced the color of summer and had dressed from head to toe in a bright-yellow track suit. Even her sneakers and daisy clip-on earrings were yellow. Thank God, Kat had her sunglasses on since looking at Mrs. D. felt like staring directly into the midday sun.

"Hey, Mrs. D., you're looking good today. Love that outfit. Is it new?"

"Yep. I ordered it online. They let me use a thirty-percent-off coupon and a free-shipping code. Quite a deal, don't cha know!" Purse (also yellow) draped over one bent, spindly arm, Mrs. D. pulled the door shut, and started speed walking—or more accurately speed shuffling—down the sidewalk.

"Are you still ordering a lot online?"

"You betcha."

Kat groaned to herself. It was great to see a senior embrace Internet shopping, but Mrs. D. never wanted to pay return shipping. So last week Kat had spent one afternoon making returns for her in person at a half dozen of Mrs. D.'s favorite stores.

"Gosh almighty! Is that your car?" Excitement shone through her cloudy cataracts.

"It is today," Kat answered with a grin, opening the passenger door. "Do you need help getting in?"

"Nope. These low cars are easy to get into." Mrs. D. lowered herself butt first into the front seat. "Might need some help getting out though."

Kat shut the door, then hustled to the driver's side and climbed in a second later. "I brought a friend along today," she said and made quick introductions.

Mrs. D. turned to look at Logan. "My goodness, you're a humdinger of a man."

Sitting knees to chin in the back, Logan started in surprise, his eyes going wide. "Umm. Thank you."

"Oh my! You have an accent too. What a fun day we're going to have, eh?" Mrs. D. clapped her hands in excitement and turned her attention to Kat. "He reminds me of my Charlie. So big and so strong and such a wonderful lover."

Hearing a sharp intake of breath behind her, Kat checked on Logan in the rearview mirror as she pulled into traffic. His handsome features registered a mixture of shock and amusement.

"Charlie didn't have hair like that though," the tiny woman continued. "My goodness, what pretty blond waves he has. Is he your boyfriend?"

"No, ma'am. I've been trying to sleep with him, but he keeps saying no." Glancing at Mrs. D., Kat gave a palms-up gesture. "I don't get it. We're both single, and he totally finds me hot."

"Maybe all his parts don't work right, eh?" Mrs. D. dropped her voice to a loud whisper.

"Hmm. I hadn't thought of that." Kat grinned at the strangled sound coming from the backseat and semi-smoothly shifted the car into third gear. "I figured he was playing hard to get. But maybe you're on to something."

"You know I can hear you, right?" Logan's deep voice rumbled with irritation.

"Oh my. Do men do that nowadays?" Mrs. D. asked, ignoring the objection from the back seat. "When I was young, I had more men chasing me than I could poke a stick at. My Charlie used to show up at my house every Saturday morning with a handful of wildflowers he picked in the woods behind his parents' house. 'Course, one morning the bunch he brought had three perfect red roses tucked in there too. He swore he didn't steal them from old Mrs. Nevenhaur's yard, but I always suspected he'd done just that." Mrs. D. chuckled at the memory then patted Kat on the arm. "Don't worry about it, dear. You just be yourself. He'll come around."

"I'm only in town for a short while," Logan explained. "I'm not getting involved because I don't want her to get hurt. Bloody noblest thing I've ever done, and all I get is shit for it," he added under his breath.

"Why do you have to leave town?" Mrs. D. asked, turning in her seat to stare him down. "And where are you going then?"

"My job here only lasts through the summer," he said, sounding a bit defensive. "Not sure where I'm going after that. Might go back to Costa Rica ... Might go somewhere new."

"Logan doesn't stick," Kat explained.

"Why not?"

"Glad you asked, Mrs. D. I've been working on a few theories about that."

"I bet you've come up with some doozies, eh?" Mrs. D's voice sounded as effervescent as her bright-yellow ensemble.

"Oh, they're doozies all right," Kat confirmed with exaggerated severity. "Wanna hear them?"

"Yeah!"

"No!"

Though Mrs. D.'s and Logan's simultaneous responses were equally passionate, Kat—not so surprisingly—ignored Logan's.

"Theory one—"

"Instead of yabbering about my flaws," Logan groused behind her. "It'd be ace if you told me where we're going and if we're going to get there before my dangly bits join both of my feet in slumber."

Kat smirked at Logan in the mirror. "No worries, mate. I'm happy to wake up your sleeping extremities when we arrive."

Logan sighed. "Where exactly is there?" he asked, totally ignoring her generous offer.

"Katherine takes me with her whenever she drives to Sheboygan to mow the yard at my friend Lillian's house. That way Lillian and I can catch up at least once a week. 'Course, I couldn't go last time because Katherine's car was too hot for me to ride in that far. I'm sure glad I could come along this time. I would have hated to miss two trips in a row."

"How often does *Katherine* help your friend?"

Kat tensed at the blatant sound of interest in Logan's voice. "My involvement doesn't matter. The important thing to note is the need to help older folks in the area."

"Oh my, let's see," Mrs. D. said, turning to Logan as if Kat hadn't said a damn thing. "She helps Lillian with shopping and odds and ends around the house whenever she mows her yard. She stops at my house to help out every Wednesday after taking me to the grocery store. And she runs some other errands for me and my other friend Margaret during the week. 'Course, now she's also taking Harry to his chiropractor appointments in Green Bay. I'm not sure how she's going to do it all now that she works at her sister's place."

Kat gave her a reassuring smile. "Don't worry. I told Hannah I could only work mornings. I'll still be able to help out in the afternoons." She could feel Logan's gaze locked on her. And not in a hot, sexy kind of way. Nope, he was sending off a smug I-know-something-you-don't-want-me-to-know vibe.

Logan remained quiet the rest of the drive. Kat wasn't sure if he was pondering what he'd learned about her or if the cramped conditions had cut off circulation to his brain. Either way, she appreciated that the conversation was no longer about her.

When she pulled to a stop in front of Lillian's small, square blue house a half hour later, Mrs. D. had just finished a long, very detailed Internet-shopping lecture on why it was better to use a free-shipping coupon over a twenty-percent-off coupon.

"We're here," Kat said, hopping from the car before Mrs. D. launched into her tirade about deceitful return policies. She hustled to the passenger side and helped pull the older woman to her feet.

"Thanks, dear. I'll go see Lillian." She patted Kat's arm before speed shuffling toward the front door.

Kat turned her attention to Logan struggling to extract himself from the tiny backseat. It took a minute—and an excessive amount of swearing—but he eventually made it out. After stretching to his full height and working out a few kinks in his neck, Logan turned his baby blues to her—a satisfied smile on his face.

"So, darl, you're a real-life superhero disguised as a badass, ay." He tucked a stray strand of hair behind her ear. "You had me fooled. Had no idea a tiger like you could have such a soft underbelly."

The middle finger seemed like the only appropriate response to his asinine comment, so that's the one she gave him. Ignoring his answering laughter, she stomped toward the tool shed to retrieve the ancient push mower.

"Soft underbelly, my ass," Kat grumbled to herself. "I bet he won't be laughing when I hit every frickin' pothole on the drive home."

EIGHT

THE next evening, sitting on a barstool in the kitchen, Kat reread Logan's text, desperately hoping she'd misunderstood it the first time.

Good news. Talked to your parents. Willing to hear more about proposal to focus program on senior citizens. Discussing with them over dinner. Don't wait up.

Her heart hammered against her rib cage and her stomach tightened into a painful knot. The last rays of sun were about to slip below the western landscape. In less than ten minutes, it would be completely dark outside, and she was sitting in the middle of frickin' nowhere by herself.

As a sheen of sweat covered her body, Kat quickly checked the locks on all of the cottage's doors and windows. She could do this. Logan wouldn't be gone for more than a few hours. She could watch a movie to pass the time. Or read a book. Or hide under her bed.

No! She had to fight against her weakness. She wouldn't cower anymore. If she didn't stand up to this ridiculous fear, it would continue to grow until it eventually controlled every aspect of her life.

Kat ground her teeth and focused on taking deep, slow breaths while she tossed a salad together for dinner. *Don't think about it. Don't frickin' think about it.* She repeated the words over and over in her head, carried her dinner to the couch, and pulled up *Guardians of the Galaxy* to watch. Not only would the awesome soundtrack and humor distract her, the movie should put her problem into perspective. She only had to hang out alone for one night; the Guardians had to save the whole universe.

With about half the movie and almost all of her salad left to finish, Kat heard the rumble of a truck engine drive up the lane and pull to a stop outside her front door. It sounded like one of those powerful diesel engines she'd heard around Bennett Industries in the past.

Holy hell. Some stranger, likely up to no good, was outside the cottage. He could break in and overpower her faster than she could call Logan or the police. And even if she did call for help, the guy could slit her throat and toss her body into the lake before anyone could get to the secluded cottage in time to stop him.

Panic dropped her heart to her toes. She fumbled with the remote to turn off the television. She needed to hide, but her hands were shaking and her fingers were so numb she kept hitting the wrong damn buttons.

Finally, she hit the power button sending the screen to black and the room into silence. And that's when she heard the heart-stopping sound of a key sliding into the lock. Whoever was outside was about to come in!

Kat grabbed the closest thing to a weapon she could find—sadly, her salad fork—braced herself for the upcoming fight, and watched in horror as the door swung open.

"Hey, tiger. Miss me?" Logan sauntered through the door with his trademark easy smile and carefree attitude. But his face tightened the second he looked her way. "What's wrong?"

In that instant, she hated him. She hated him for leaving her alone at night and for scaring the shit out of her. She hated him for seeing her like this: afraid, vulnerable, pathetic. Most of all, she hated him for being so damn strong that he could live without fear controlling his life.

Logan would never taste the metallic residue fear left behind in his mouth. Fear would never dominate his thoughts or control his actions. Fear would never hollow him from the inside while it fed on itself, growing stronger as it made him weaker. He would never know the crushing weight of fear or its ability to twist and warp you into a pathetic, useless version of your former self.

She was weak. He was strong. And she hated him for it.

But she hated herself even more.

The fork slipped from her hand and clanked against the wood floor as the fight drained from her. Kat knew she should feel relieved and grateful to see him, or even angry and embarrassed. Instead, she only felt numb and tired.

She didn't even try to remain standing when her knees gave out. She was so drained she didn't care if she landed on the couch or the floor. She sank only a few inches, however, before two strong hands caught her shoulders and hauled her back to her feet.

"Look at me," Logan demanded.

The unexpected tension in his voice caught her attention more than his words. Only inches away, he stood directly in front of her, his hands still tightly gripping each of her shoulders.

"How'd you get from there," she said, nodding to the little foyer, "to here so quickly?"

"I thought you were going to pass out, so I hurdled the damn couch. What the hell is wrong?"

"Nothing's wrong," she answered, feeling oddly distanced from the whole conversation.

"Bullshit. You're ghostly pale, shaking under my hands, and sound like a damn zombie." He sounded royally pissed off. He must have thought the same thing because he drew in a deep breath and blew it out slowly. "What happened to make you so scared?" he asked in a slightly calmer voice.

She huffed out a humorless laugh. "Do you mean tonight or in the past?"

"Both."

She'd never told anyone about the incident in DC that had sent her running back to Wisconsin almost a year ago. She'd been too ashamed of her weakness to admit it before, but now—drained of all emotions—she only felt numb. "Tonight," she said, turning her head to stare blindly out the window, "I heard a truck I didn't recognize."

"I borrowed a truck from your dad's company, so I could take Lillian's old mower in for a tune-up."

She locked her arms around her chest. "I thought someone was breaking into the cottage."

"Crooks don't usually have keys."

"I wasn't thinking straight. I don't ... " She paused and swallowed hard, trying to dislodge the lump forming in her throat. "I don't like to be alone at night."

He cocked his head in confusion. "Why not?"

Refusing to look at him, Kat clenched her jaw closed and shook her head. She didn't want to talk about it. She didn't even want to think about it.

"Tell me, or I'll haul your butt to your parents' house and tell them what's going on." He shrugged. "It's your choice, but they'll probably insist on attending multiple lengthy, emotion-baring therapy sessions with you."

"I don't need therapy, jerkface." Kat shoved his big chest with both hands. "I just need to move on. Talking to you while we braid each other's hair isn't going to help."

A smile tugged at his cheeks. "There's the fire. I was starting to worry it had all burnt out."

His thumb grazed down her cheek with so much tenderness she should have made fun of him for it. But her defenses were down, and honestly, it felt nice to have someone care.

"How about we sit down and you tell me the short version of what happened? If you don't want to say anything else after that, I won't push you for more details. Fair?"

With a massive eye roll, Kat dropped her butt to the couch. "Fine. Let's make this quick." As soon as Logan sat down on the chair beside her, she launched into a bare-bones description of the night that changed her life. "I used to walk alone at night in DC all the time."

"Shit," Logan mumbled, bracing his elbows on

his knees and scrubbing a hand down his face. "I'm going to hate this story."

Kat took in his rigid body and uneasy expression and let out a dramatic sigh. "Relax. Nothing horrible happened. Some asshole took my bag and ran off. End of story." She left out the ugliest details to save them both the discomfort of it. She figured her simplified version would appease his curiosity, and he'd let the subject drop.

If anything, Logan's expression looked even tenser. Actually, he was grinding his teeth so hard he looked about ten levels past tense. "Did he hurt you?"

She shook her head, not wanting to go there. "It doesn't matter."

Logan balled his hands into fists. "Did he fucking touch you?" he asked, his voice low and rough.

Kat flinched at the vivid memory his question triggered: the nauseating feel of a filthy forearm shoved into her throat, pinning her against the rough brick wall. It had left a nasty bruise on her neck for a couple of weeks, an unwanted visual reminder of the asshole who mugged her.

Breaking eye contact, Kat dropped her gaze to her lap. "I only had one block to go before my apartment. I thought I was alone." She sucked in a deep breath and tried to distance herself from the memory. No frickin' way was she going to tear up in front of Logan. "I didn't hear him come up behind me. I had no idea he was there until he grabbed me and pulled me into an alley beside the building. He pushed his arm into my throat to hold me against the wall while he said some disgusting things and dug through my pockets. When he heard a group of people turn onto the block, he grabbed my bag and took off." She sniffled a little, shrugged, and returned her gaze to his. "I'd been an idiot to walk alone at night. I was lucky nothing worse happened. At least, that's what the police told me."

"Lucky? You were attacked, and they said you were lucky? Un-fucking-believable. Did they catch the bastard?"

"No. They said it happened more often than people realized and that I shouldn't go out alone at night anymore."

"So now you don't feel safe if you're alone at night anywhere," Logan said evenly.

"Pretty dumb, huh?" Kat scoffed. "I'm a grown woman who's afraid of the dark." Tears began to fill her eyes, and her throat tightened. She sniffed, swallowed roughly, and blinked her eyes like crazy, hoping to stop the waterworks before they really got going.

"Oh, tiger, don't cry." Logan moved to sit beside her on the couch. He wrapped his muscular arm around her and pulled her tight to his side, dropping a kiss on the top of her head.

Burying her head in his solid chest, she drew in a deep breath. He smelled frickin' amazing, like a spicy citrus soap mixed with warm male skin. She had the sudden urge to lick his neck. *Huh?* Who knew lust could chase away sadness so quickly? She snuggled up and sucked in another intoxicating lungful.

Logan pulled her closer and kissed the top of her head again. "It's okay. You're safe now. Just don't cry."

She grinned against his chest. He must have

thought she was fighting back a runny nose rather than getting drunk on his scent. God, she needed help. Logan was trying to comfort her, and her mind went straight to the sex. Clearly, he was the bigger person in more ways than one.

"I'm fine now. I'm not going to cry." She pulled back with a sigh. "Thanks for listening. I've never admitted that to anyone before."

"Admitted what?"

"You know ... taking stupid risks. Thinking nothing bad would ever happen to me. Feeling like I could take care of any situation that came up. My family would freak if they knew what I did."

Tipping her chin up, Logan forced her to meet his eyes. "You didn't do anything. Something shitty was done to you." Rubbing his thumb along her jawline, he held her gaze.

Kat's heart zoomed into overdrive, kicking up her breathing a few notches. Her mouth slipped open to compensate for the sudden need for more oxygen.

Logan's eyes darkened as his gaze dropped to her lips. With excruciating slowness, he drew his thumb across her bottom lip. "So bloody soft," he murmured before dropping his hand away.

Instinct driving her, Kat leaned forward and brushed her lips against his.

He froze.

Hoping like hell he didn't pull away, Kat kissed him again and pressed herself against his body. A shudder ran through him, and then—thank God— he kissed her back.

Logan's kiss eclipsed even the most vivid of her fantasies. As his mouth moved slowly, thoroughly, over hers, all thoughts of the past flew from her mind. Her only semi-coherent thought being that no one had ever kissed her with the same mesmerizing mixture of tenderness and desire.

His taste on her lips, his body pressed to hers, and the low groan of need sounding from the back of his throat heated her blood and scorched her senses. Kat ached for more and tried to send him the message by moaning and pushing harder against him. Either Logan didn't understand, or he chose to ignore her. He continued the slow exploration of her mouth—nipping, teasing, tasting at a leisurely pace, and quickly driving her crazy with desire.

Sliding a hand into her hair, he tilted her head to the side, allowing access to the sensitive nerves along her neck. He trailed warm, wet kisses down the exposed expanse of skin, pausing to unhurriedly nip and suck the spot under the corner of her jawbone. Her nipples tightened while the rest of her throbbed.

"Why is it that the slower you go, the faster you make me want you to go?" Kat said, squirming in his arms. "Is that part of your master plan?"

She felt his grin against her neck. "Darl, with you there is no plan. No, scratch that. There is a plan, but I can't seem to stick to it." Shaking his head, he let go of her, and rose to his feet. "Living with you is like walking across the bloody Outback with an ice-cold bottle of water that I'm not allowed to drink."

"Thanks," she responded with a smile.

"It wasn't a compliment." He grimaced. "I can't figure out if you're my punishment or my reward."

"Um. Thank you?"

"Again. Not a compliment."

"It kinda sounded like one." She shrugged. "Just

to be clear, does that whole Outback-water-bottle analogy mean we aren't going to have sex tonight, or are you just thirsty?"

Logan's eyes narrowed and a low rumble of frustration rose from the back of his throat. "We are not having sex tonight."

He towered over her, breathing heavily and clenching his fists. Damn, frustrated looked frickin' sexy on him.

Kat tipped her head to the side. "Why not?"

"Because you're vulnerable, so it would be the wrong thing to do. And for some bloody reason, I can't get past that."

Kat swallowed a laugh. "This is a real low point for you, huh?"

He shoved a hand through his hair. "You have no idea," he muttered.

"Would it really be so bad to take one little sip of water from that bottle? Might be all it takes to quench your thirst."

"Or I might drain it in one gulp and still need more. You wanna risk it?"

The burning look in Logan's eye crackled with an intensity that immediately silenced her. Waves of desire, frustration, and a quickly fading restraint poured off of his tensed body.

She sat wide-eyed and frozen to the spot. What the hell did he mean by that? Kat opened her mouth, but no words came out.

A humorless smile lifted one corner of his mouth. "Yeah. I didn't think so."

She heard Logan pass behind her and go into his room. She waited to hear his door close and the lock click into place, but neither sound ever came. She didn't know if he'd done it intentionally, but leaving his door open soothed her nerves. For the first time since the mugging, she went to bed that night with her own bedroom door unlocked and wide open.

Lying in bed, feeling both nervous and excited by the small step, Kat promised herself that tomorrow night she would try sleeping with her bedroom window cracked open an inch.

Even baby steps could eventually lead the way to normal, right?

NINE

"WHERE are we going, and why am I not driving?"

Shifting the car into fourth, Logan looked over at Kat sitting beside him in a stretchy black workout outfit. She seemed more curious than irritated by his mysterious invitation to join him for the day.

"We're going to Milwaukee, and you aren't driving because the last time I let you get behind the wheel, you hit every blasted pothole in the road. On purpose."

She laughed. "Fair point."

It had been almost a week since he'd come home to find her frozen, pale, and death-gripping a salad fork in the living room. When she'd told him about the attack, he'd nearly gone crazy with rage. Even now, he wanted to rip the bastard's head off and probably would if he ever found him.

But today was about being prepared, not getting even. He just hoped the decision to keep this a secret from Kat didn't turn out to be a major mistake. He knew it was a risky move. Hell, she might refuse to participate, but he still had to try something. He couldn't stand the thought of ever seeing her so scared and vulnerable again. And like it or not, he wouldn't always be there to protect her.

"So why did I have to wear comfortable clothes today?" She frowned. "I should be dressed a little nicer if we're heading into the city."

He blew out a breath and glanced her way. "I'll tell you where we're going. But you have to promise not to permanently damage any of my favorite body parts."

She narrowed her eyes. "No way I'm making that promise. Spill it, McCabe. What did you do?"

He turned his attention back to the road, trying like hell to look casual. "I signed you up for a day-long women's self-defense class. Even though you don't have to attend, I hope you'll consider it," he added quickly before she could argue. "You can't let the assholes of the world stop you from living, but I'd feel better knowing you can beat the shit out of any guy that bothers you again."

"What if you're the guy bothering me?"

He chuckled. "Then you should definitely beat the shit out of me."

"This class will teach me how?" She sounded intrigued.

"Too right."

"Okay, big guy." She clicked her tongue. "I'll do it."

"Should I be worried by how happy you sound right now?"

"Too right," she said, mimicking his accent.

He grimaced. "Remember, you promised not to damage any parts that won't recover."

"Actually, I remember *not* making that promise. Don't worry, though, I'm not mad. I've been thinking about taking a class like this since the night it happened." She turned to look out the window. "But every time I thought about looking for one, it brought back memories I wanted to forget."

Cursing under his breath, Logan let up on the accelerator. "I'm sorry, darl. I'm a no-hoper." He should have realized this would bring back memories of the attack. "It's too soon. I'll take you home."

"No." She put her hand on his arm and paused, waiting for him to glance at her. "I want to do this. I need to do this."

"That's ace," he mumbled, trying to ignore his reaction to her touch. Kat didn't need a horny bloke to deal with today. "If you'd like, I could also teach you how to lift weights to add a few pounds of muscle. I know that might not be enough to take down a guy who outweighs you by a hundred pounds, but it could help you get away."

"Actually, I'd like that a lot. My gym isn't close, so I don't get there very often. Plus, I don't know how most of the machines work or what weight I should be using. I usually just hop on the elliptical for as long as I can stand the boredom, then head home."

"That's pretty typical. A lot of people get stuck in the same exercise routine because they don't know what else to do. And when they do try something new, their form usually sucks. They can end up hurting themselves."

"Sounds like you know a lot about this."

"My mum got me a job at a country club when I was younger. Working in the fitness center was one of the things I did there."

"Is your mom still in Australia?"

"Yip. After I finished school, she married a bloke with three boys. They all live outside of Sydney." He grinned. "Sounds like the boys are real hell-raisers. Mum said they make raising me seem like a walk in the park."

"I like them already." Kat chuckled. "Do you visit often?"

"Nah. They don't need me around. Mum has plenty of help taking out the rubbish now."

"Need? No. But I'm sure they'd want you around." Kat shifted in her seat to stare at him. "Did you help your mom a lot growing up?"

"It was just the two of us. As soon as I was big enough, I took care of the stuff requiring any muscle since Mum's just a bit of a thing. She took care of everything else." He shrugged a shoulder. "She had it rough raising a kid alone. I did what I could to help but still wish I could have done more."

"So how'd you get from Australia to Costa Rica?"

"After Mum got married, I landed a job on a cruise ship."

"Seriously, you worked on a cruise ship?" Kat laughed. "I don't picture you fitting into one of those tiny bunks below deck."

He grinned. "Since I had a certification in personal training, they hired me to oversee the fitness program on the ship. The job came with a slightly larger cabin."

"I bet the single women looking to make memories on their vacations loved you. Do I even want to know how many of them you hooked up with during your time at sea, sailor?"

He gripped the wheel and pretended to concentrate on the traffic in front of him, hating the reminder that women didn't want or need a guy like him around for long. "It wasn't that many."

Kat grunted. "To you maybe. So you've worked as a fitness trainer, adventure travel guide, a surf instructor, and you helped Pax run the social outreach program at La Vida. Anything else important I should know about?"

"Nope. I got on a cruise ship in Australia, and I got off in South America. I bounced around there for a while, then headed north. Stayed in Costa Rica for a while after meeting Pax." He shrugged. "Came here after that."

"Sounds like the abridged version of a very colorful story," Kat said. "I won't push for more info since the full details might send me into cardiac arrest. Change of subject. Any updates on Bennett Industries' fledgling community outreach program?"

"As soon as your mum and dad agreed to focus the program on the elderly, things have started taking shape."

"That's great! There's a limit to the number of yards I can mow every week. How do you plan to round up volunteers?"

"I've got an idea, but I wanted to run it by you since you're from here and know better than I do whether it will fly."

"Shoot."

"I've heard the local high school requires all senior students to perform volunteer work before they graduate. What if we partnered with the school? The students could come to us when they had hours to fill, and we could match them up with an older person who's requested help. Hopefully, some of the kids would enjoy the work enough to continue helping out after they've filled their requirement." He shifted his gaze to Kat. "If it's done right, the students might even learn a thing or two from the old folks."

"I love it." She grinned. "You could call it Seniors Assisting Seniors or S-A-S. But let's pronounce it like the word 'sass.' It has a nice ring to it."

"With a name like that, you should be running it," he teased.

"I've got enough on my plate. But I'm happy to help …" She paused, pulling her phone from her bag. "I'll text a friend who works at the school." She punched the screen for a minute then tucked the phone away. "Done. I'll let you know what he says."

"He?" Logan grunted, the gender of Kat's friend irritating him more than it should.

"John Vornado. He's a counselor at the high school. We graduated together."

"Is that all you did together?" he asked dryly, looking her way.

"Nope."

"What else did you and John do together?"

"Nothing much. Nothing that I'm not willing to do with you." She winked at him. "Why? You jealous?"

"No," he snapped.

"Really? 'Cause you look a little jealous."

Logan growled under his breath, flexed his fingers, and re-gripped the wheel. "New topic." Just because he hated the thought of Kat with another guy didn't make him jealous.

"Okay. Fine." She laughed. "Tell me what else you're doing at work while we wait for John to respond."

"Trish and I are looking for a few full-time employees to bring on board. We need a small staff to turn it over to once I leave."

"Trish? As in Trisha Thumble, the perky blonde who works in the legal department?"

"Yeah, your dad asked her to help me get things up and running. Once the groundwork is laid, she'll return to legal work."

"Careful, big guy. I've known Trisha for years. No way she'll return to working on briefs without attempting to get into yours first."

He stifled a grin. "I appreciate your concern, but Trish isn't my type."

"You have a type now?" Kat asked, turning to study him. "When did that happen? I thought you were an equal opportunity seducer of female hearts."

Damn. She had a point. He'd never been picky about women. Trish had a cute face and curvy body that he would have taken interest in not that long ago, but he hadn't thought twice about her. Nope. All of his thoughts were stubbornly, idiotically focused on the spitfire sitting next to him.

Maybe it was a case of wanting what he couldn't have. The cramp in his arse suggested the attraction had more to do with her sharp wit, quick smile, unfiltered comments, and the soft heart she tried to hide behind a tough exterior.

No doubt about it. Kat was complicated, and he'd avoided complicated for years. Simple suited him better. Simple equaled fun. Simple meant walking away without regrets or guilt. No one got hurt when relationships remained simple.

"So what's your type?" Kat prodded.

"Simple."

"You like simple women? As in simpleminded?" she asked, her tone a mixture of pity and disbelief. "Or do you mean easy instead of simple? Is this one of those Australian-English to American-English translation issues? Because I definitely see easy women as being right up your alley."

He tightened his grip on the wheel. "I didn't mean simple women or easy women. I like simple relationships."

"I hate to break it to you, big guy, but if it's simple, it ain't a relationship. Relationships are complicated, painful, and sometimes so frickin' frustrating you want to run the opposite direction screaming obscenities at the top of your lungs. And that's not the worst part." Kat snorted. "The real rub is relationships can also make you feel so damn great you start to believe they're actually worth all the horrible shit they put you through in the first place."

He grimaced and rubbed a painful knot at the back of his neck. "Christ, if that's true then we've been in a relationship since the day we first crashed together."

"Yep," Kat agreed cheerfully. "But you've locked that chastity belt of yours so tight we haven't been able to enjoy the fringe benefit of unlimited orgasms."

Chuckling, he looked her way. "You're relentless."

She flashed him a cheeky smile. "It's one of my best qualities."

"That's debatable."

"Really? Which of my many qualities would you debate to be my best?"

"Tough call. Maybe your modesty. Or your mild temperament." He looked at her out of the corner of his eye. "No wait, it has to be the way you've showered me with warm, gentle affection."

"Damn, big guy, you're right." She slugged him hard on the shoulder. "I'm a real catch!"

"Ouch." He rubbed his bicep. "For a little thing, you pack a big punch."

"After today it'll be even bigger. Hey look, John texted back." Kat studied her phone for a beat. "When will we be home tonight?"

"Probably by five. Why?" he asked, turning into an industrial park on the northern end of Milwaukee.

"I want to talk to John about SAS. It would help to have him on board." Kat typed a quick response. "It's all set. I'm meeting him for dinner tonight. It shouldn't be hard convincing him it's a great idea. I can be *very* persuasive."

The thought of Kat using her powers of persuasion on some other guy shot his blood pressure into the red zone. "I'll come along in case he has any questions you can't answer," he said, pulling to a stop in front of a single-story beige building.

"Sorry, big guy, I haven't needed a chaperone since I was fifteen and Dad made Hannah sit between me and Gabe Leyden at the movie theater." She tapped her window, pointing to the building. "Is this the place?"

"Yeah. Do you want me to come in with you?"

"Nope. I've got this." She started to get out of

the car, paused, then turned back to him, her expression suddenly serious. "Thanks for doing this, Logan. No matter what I've said in the past or what I'm bound to say in the future—you really are a great guy." She kissed his cheek and went inside.

He was left speechless and more than a little worried about the uncomfortable tightness in the region of his heart.

•••

Kat slipped into a pair of slim-fitting jeans, an airy white peasant top, and a kick-ass pair of glossy red wedge sandals. She finger combed the long, loose waves of her hair, leaving it to fall freely around her shoulders. She played up the slight slant of her eyes with dark eyeshadow, black eyeliner, and a touch of mascara. One dollop of dark red lip gloss and her favorite faux snakeskin clutch later, and she was ready for her date with John.

To be fair, John had not been on her mind while she'd been getting ready. Nope. The flirty outfit, sexy shoes, and smokin' makeup were for Logan's benefit. Right or wrong, she wanted to see the same mind-blowing desire in his eyes as the night they'd kissed. Just the memory of it made her best parts tingle.

"Get a grip." She shook her head. John was picking her up any minute. If she opened the door looking all hot-and-bothered, he might get the wrong idea and go running for the hills. Even though she'd insinuated that she and John had been romantically involved in the past, they hadn't. He was a great guy and a good friend, nothing more. She didn't plan to clarify the situation with her iron-willed roommate anytime soon.

She should probably cut Logan some slack since he'd been a real sweetheart today. Taking her to that self-defense class, waiting around Milwaukee for five hours, then driving her home, all went above and beyond his duties as a roommate or as her brother's best friend.

The class had been great. Not that she'd learned everything she ever needed to know about protecting herself in one day, but she felt stronger and a little more confident now. She'd even signed up to take additional classes when her instructor offered to solidify and expand on the defense techniques she'd learned.

Three quick knocks on the front door pulled her thoughts to the here and now. She checked her reflection one last time, hustled from her room, and immediately locked gazes with Logan, who looked royally peeved.

He was sitting on a barstool, leaning his elbows on the island with a glass of what smelled like scotch dangling from his fingertips. He scanned her body. His eyes flashed with heat, then immediately hardened. "No bloody way I'm answering the door for your dates."

She smothered a grin, trailing her hand along his shoulder on her way to the door. "Come on, big guy, don't sulk. A girl's ego can only take so many noes before she's gotta refuel with a yes or two."

"I don't sulk."

She shot Logan a skeptical look and swung the door open. "Hey, handsome. Long time, no see." She stretched to her tiptoes and pecked John on the cheek.

"Hi, Kat." John gave her a boyish smile. "You look great."

She clicked her tongue and winked. "You too." She hadn't seen him in a while, but his good looks had only improved with age. His dark hair and eyes were from his Latino father, his wide smile and sculpted features came from his Scandinavian mother, and his light-brown skin was a perfect mixture of the two.

"This place is great. When did you move in?" Glancing over her shoulder, his eyes widened in surprise. "Or should I ask, who did you move in with?"

Kat didn't have to turn around to know Logan had ambled over to stand behind her. Her body always hummed with awareness when he was close. And right now, if he got any closer, they'd be spooning.

"Logan. John," she said, pointing at each guy as way of introduction.

In the silence that followed, she felt their gazes clashing over her head. She looked at one guy, then the other, rolled her eyes, and elbowed Logan hard in the gut.

He grunted, then nodded once at John. "G'day, mate."

Kat scrunched her nose and looked over her shoulder. What the hell was he up to? He'd just used the thickest Australian accent she'd ever heard.

"Good to meet you," John said after a brief pause. "Australian?"

"Yip."

Good Lord, he looked smug.

"That was an observation, not a compliment,"

she drawled.

"It's never been a complaint." The rumble of his low voice only inches from her ear shot a smokin' hot shiver of desire down her spine. She ground her teeth together and fought back the urge to shove John out the door and physically throw herself against Logan's hard body.

Ugh. She couldn't do this any longer. She couldn't live in this near-constant state of arousal.

It was too damn frustrating!

She'd thought she could persuade Logan into forgetting that stupid promise to her dad, but even she had a breaking point. And if she continued to crash with Logan, she might slide across the fine line separating optimistic from delusional.

Oh, who was she kidding? She'd been hopscotching back and forth across that line since the day she set her sights on Logan McCabe.

In her defense, she'd mistaken him for a carefree pretty boy with loose morals at the time. As it turned out, his kind heart and generous nature were better suited for the long run than for a short-term love 'em-and-leave 'em deal. But—and this was a really big but—he didn't stick with anyone for the long run!

Christ, Logan drove her nuts! He acknowledged the crazy, constant attraction between them. But he refused to indulge in the present for fear of hurting her in the future because he wouldn't even consider building a life with anyone. How could a man be so right, so wrong, so great, and so frickin' annoying all at the same time?

Boiling over with frustration, Kat grabbed John's arm and shoved him toward the door. "Let's go."

His brows shot up. "Oh-kay," he said, eyeing her with curiosity. "You all right?"

"Absolutely. Just anxious to spend time with an old friend," she ground out, dragging John through the door behind her.

"Kat," Logan called to her.

"Huh?"

"Don't be afraid to use what you learned today."

"I'm sure that won't be necessary," she snapped. "Bye, *roomie*. Don't wait up."

TEN

MIDNIGHT. It was goddamn midnight before Kat strolled through the front door with a smug, sleepy, content-as-hell expression on her face.

"Where have you been?" Logan demanded. "Nothing in Silver Bay is open this late. For Christ's sake, Kat, I texted you. Twice."

She looked at him like he'd just sprouted a second head. "I muted my phone. I hate when people spend more time texting then talking." She pulled her phone from her purse. "What did you text me about? Is something wrong?"

He grunted.

A smile played around her lips as she scanned her messages. "Oh, big guy, you were worried about me?"

He grunted again.

Chuckling, she sat down next to him on the couch, dropped her head to his shoulder, and patted his knee. "Your concern is kinda sweet, but I've known John for years. He's a good guy."

"John wasn't my concern."

He felt more than heard her laughter. "Ah, I get it. You thought I'd be a bad influence on him."

"Even good guys can be tempted into making bad decisions. And you, tiger, are one giant temptation."

"I went out with John to talk about SAS, not to seduce him."

Tension eased from his body.

"But, I'll admit, I considered it for a minute."

And the tension rushed back in. He shook his head and rubbed the back of his neck with one hand. "Do I want to hear this?"

"Nothing happened." She sighed. "But I've been so sexually frustrated lately, it crossed my mind to ask John to ... you know ... do me a favor."

"He bloody well better not do you any *favors*."

"Jeez, calm down. I didn't do it. It didn't seem right to ask when you're the one I want. But, Logan, I can't stay here much longer. I need to find somewhere else to live before I self-combust. Oddly, getting to know you—I mean, really know you—has made me want you more, not less." She shrugged. "That's never happened to me before."

His chest tightened. He should encourage her to move out. It would be better for them both. But he couldn't bring himself to do it. He wasn't ready to let her go. He dropped his arm around her and pulled her slender curves to his side.

"I don't want you to leave. And that"—he sighed—"is a rarity for me too."

"So where does that leave us?"

"Screwed," he muttered.

"*Hmph.* I wish." She twisted to look at him, her

blue-gray eyes imploring and serious. "I like you, Logan. You're funny, sweet, hot, and you put up with my shit. When you leave for Costa Rica or Africa or Antarctica, or wherever you decide to go, I'm going to miss you—whether we've had sex or not."

"It'll be harder if we've slept together," he said, tucking a strand of hair behind her ear.

"Not for me. We've become friends, Logan. If we spend time together naked or not, I'll miss you all the same."

He blew out another, even bigger, sigh. "I'm trying to not hurt you."

"You won't." She placed her hand on his chest, stretched toward him, and softly kissed his lips.

He didn't react. If he did, he feared the last of his resistance would evaporate faster than water in the Outback. Instead, he clenched his jaw and fought back his desire—a damn hard thing to do, considering he wanted her more than his next breath.

She chuckled. "Man, you're tense. Are you afraid I'm going to fall in love with you? Well, I'll let you in on a little intel, big guy. I'm not going to fall for you because we have sex—even if it's the best sex in the world. If I ever fall in love with a guy, it will be because of his big heart not his big ... well, you know." She winked.

"Kat." He sounded like a man begging for his life. And in some ways that was exactly how he felt.

She must have sensed him weakening. Going in for the kill, she leaned in to trail hot, wet kisses up his jaw. "We won't regret it," she murmured only inches from his ear. "The only regret we'll have is not doing it sooner." She nipped his earlobe and shattered his control.

Letting out a growl, he scooped Kat onto his lap—her knees straddling his hips. "Didn't know I could want anyone this bloody much." He gripped her hip with one hand, slid the other into her hair, and pulled her mouth roughly to his—pouring all of his lust and frustration into the kiss.

Kat responded with the same ferocity. Moaning into his mouth, she ground her hips against him and returned his kiss with passion, desperation, and a near-violent level of need.

After a few minutes, she grabbed the edge of his shirt and yanked up. "Too many clothes," she murmured, breaking the kiss long enough to strip first his shirt and then hers.

Still straddling him, she now only wore a tight pair of jeans, a white lacy bra, her red heels, and a sexy smile. "I've been wanting to do that for a long time."

Painfully hard and mesmerized by her barely-covered breasts, eye-level and only inches away, Logan swallowed hard. "Not as long as I've wanted to do this." Feeling like he was about to open the best frigging present in the world, he slowly undid the front clasp of her bra and pulled the lacy fabric away to uncover two perfect breasts.

He ground his teeth and fought against his desperate need. He couldn't get enough of her. He had to touch her, taste her, feel her—warm and wet—wrapped around him.

He drew in a deep breath, cupped a full breast in each hand, and rubbed the rough pads of his thumbs over her tight, pert nipples.

Kat threw her head back and arched. "God, don't stop," she panted, sending her breasts closer to his face.

Unable to resist the invitation, he licked and sucked one of her perfect nipples while he rolled the other between his thumb and forefinger. He continued toying with her breasts, moving his mouth from one hardened peak to the other, wanting her as desperate with need as she made him.

She gasped and squirmed, rubbing against him while she gripped his hair to hold him pinned to her breasts. "In me," she panted, circling her hips again and again. "I need you in me."

He grinned at her half-demanding and half-begging tone. She finally sounded as frantic as he felt. He set her on her feet, undid her jeans, and peeled them and her lacy underwear off. A second later, his pants joined the pile of clothing on the cottage floor.

Kissing her again, he backed her to the kitchen island.

"We're going the wrong way," she panted. "The bedroom is behind you."

"Can't make it that far." He nipped her neck. "Besides, condoms are out here." He lifted her hips and sat her warm, naked body onto the counter-height granite.

"You keep condoms in our kitchen?"

"You never know when you're going to need one." He grinned, stepping between her widespread legs. He caught her mouth with his again, gripped one of her thighs, and used his other hand to trace a finger along her heated center. He slid two fingers into her and groaned as she cried out in pleasure again. He withdrew, quickly pushed back inside then curved his fingers to rub the sensitive spot deep inside of her.

Kat writhed, squirmed, and panted in front of him. She was so damn beautiful his gut ached. Bracing her arms behind her, she dropped her head back and thrust against his fingers. "You," she panted. "Logan, I want *you* inside of me."

"Just to be clear, tiger, is this you asking me to take *it* out of my pants? Because you said that was never gonna happen."

"Dammit, Logan. Don't make me hurt you."

Grinning, he pulled his fingers from her, reached into the end drawer, and withdrew a foil packet from the back. He kicked off his boxer-briefs, rolled the condom on, and positioned himself at her core. He gripped her hips in both hands and looked at Kat.

His heart stuttered to a stop. Her beautiful blue-gray eyes were wide and locked on the hardened length of him about to push into her.

"You're big. I mean … bigger than I expected." She gulped and looked up, apprehension marring her expression.

Oh, shit. His chest tightened. "Do you want to stop?" he asked, stepping back and trying like hell to hide both the strain in his voice and the tension coursing through him.

"No." She wrapped her legs around his waist. "No frickin' way are we stopping. Just know that I talk a big game but really haven't been up to bat that often." She pulled him closer with her legs. "So maybe you could start off easy rather than a fastball down the pipe. Okay?"

Laughter rumbled through his chest. Incredible.

Even while desire scorched his blood and panic knotted his stomach, Kat could make him laugh.

She narrowed her eyes. "Something funny, big guy?"

Logan ran a hand up her thigh and rested it on her hip. "If you're going to use sports analogies with me," he said, pausing for a moment to lean forward and explore her lips in a slow, thorough kiss. "You should probably use rugby or soccer terms." He nibbled her neck, focusing on the tender spot under the corner of her jaw until she panted and squirmed beneath him again.

"Like scrum and offside?" she murmured, sounding distracted. "Those don't sound very sexy." She dug her fingers into his shoulders and urged him closer.

Chuckling, he trailed kisses down her body, taking a long, leisurely time to nibble and suck all the interesting parts along the way. When he reached the apex between her thighs, he looked up into her eyes. "How about charge-down? Does that sound sexy enough for you?"

"Charge-down?"

"Yip. Rugby term that could be used to describe one of my specialties." He dropped to a knee, placed one palm on each of her thighs, and gently pushed her legs apart.

She gave him a wicked grin. "Hmm. Never heard of it. Maybe you could demonstrate?"

"Love to, darl." Leaning forward, his own wicked grin in place, Logan *demonstrated* with his mouth until Kat writhed and thrashed wildly on the slick countertop in front of him.

"Okay." Sliding her hands into his hair, she

pulled him up and sucked in a deep breath. "Let's do this. Now."

"Are you sure?"

"Absolutely." She vice-gripped his biceps with her hands and locked her legs around his waist.

His own body rigid, Logan called on the last threads of his restraint and positioned himself at her center. Holding a slender thigh in each hand, he began to slowly work into her, pausing after each inch slid deeper, giving her time to adjust to his size. Eyes shut, Kat squirmed and let loose a few curses but didn't ask him to stop.

Finally, he was completely inside of her. Unable to breathe, he held himself still and watched her reaction. "Are you okay, tiger?"

Biting her lip, her eyes fluttered open. "I'm more than okay." She tentatively rotated her hips. "Damn, big guy, you really deserve your nickname."

His ability to breathe finally returned when she flashed him another sexy smile.

"It's a gift and a curse," he teased as he began to move inside of her.

"Feels like a gift to me," she murmured and pulled his mouth to hers.

The kiss was hot, hard, and so damn passionate, he couldn't think of anything other than how great she made him feel. Her warm body, sweet scent, and addictive taste surrounded him. He couldn't get enough. He withdrew and slid back into her as she moaned into his mouth. He did it again, only harder, and this time she broke off the kiss.

"More. Please, Logan, I'm ready for more."

Her plea snapped his restraint. He pounded into her tight, wet heat until every nerve in his body screamed with the need for release. When he couldn't stand the tormenting pleasure a second longer, Logan lowered his hand and circled his thumb over the bundle of nerves at her core. Kat dug her nails into his shoulders, arched her back, and tensed. An instant later, screaming in release, she flew over the edge.

With the feel of her body spasming around him, Logan slammed into her one final time and came in the hardest, most intense frigging orgasm of his life.

•••

Eyes closed, body sated, and mind blissfully hazy, Kat purred as Logan scooped her off the countertop and carried her to his bedroom. She had no idea how the man had the strength to walk, let alone carry her, after that workout. When he laid her on the bed, she stretched her arms over her head and managed to peel her eyes open.

Standing over her, slick with sweat, hair rumpled and gloriously naked, Logan looked so damn hot she wanted him again. At least her mind did. Drained of all energy, her body needed recharging before it could do anything remotely strenuous.

"Take a load off. You earned it." She grinned and patted the empty space beside her.

Logan scanned her body from head to toe and then back to head again. He shoved a hand through his surfer-boy hair, muttered a curse, and strode from the room.

"Huh?" Kat propped herself on her elbows and stared at the empty door. "Guess you're not feeling as relaxed as I am," she called to the other room.

A moment later, Logan returned. Still shirtless, he'd pulled his jeans on but left the zipper and snap of his fly distractingly open. Eyes focused on the prize, Kat didn't notice the fuzzy red throw blanket in his hand until he tossed it over her.

"Did I look chilly?" she asked.

"We need to talk, and I can't think straight when you're naked." He began pacing the small room refusing to meet her gaze. "Are you sure—"

"Yes," she interrupted with a grin.

He stopped pacing and looked at her. "You didn't let me finish. When I tell women I'm only good for the short-term, they tend to think they can change my mind. It's like I've issued some sort of challenge."

She shrugged one shoulder. "I'm not interested in changing you."

Shaking his head, Logan kind of sighed and kind of laughed. "Never met a woman like you before."

"Thanks." She clicked her tongue and winked. "You're pretty darn special yourself."

He raised an eyebrow. "So … you and me, we're okay?"

She gave a throaty laugh. "Oh, big guy, we're way better than okay. We were frickin' phenomenal. Of course, you may be a one-hit-wonder," she added, tilting her head and studying him with an exaggerated expression of consideration. "For all I know, the charge-down is the only really great move you've got."

"Tiger, all my moves are ace."

Amazingly, Logan's deep, gravelly voice stirred to life the parts of her body he'd just completely exhausted.

"Yeah?" she asked, peeling the blanket away and chucking it to the floor. "Prove it."

His eyes flared and a wicked grin lifted the corners of his mouth. "Glad to, darl."

By three in the morning, Logan had utterly convinced Kat of his exceptional abilities. But that didn't stop her from demanding more proof at five and then again at eight. After all, there was nothing wrong with conducting a very thorough investigation.

ELEVEN

KAT pulled her car to a stop alongside Hannah's efficient sedan and Claire's luxury SUV. Par for the course, both of her sisters had beat her to Sunday-night dinner at their parents' house. Before climbing out, she touched up her makeup and smoothed down her hair, then checked her reflection in the rearview mirror.

Damn. Her smug smile, languid expression, and glowing skin embodied the look of a thoroughly satisfied woman.

No way would her dad ever notice, but her mom was incredibly perceptive. If she walked in to the family dinner looking all Kat-that-got-the-cream content, her mom would be on to her in a second. Yeah, she'd told her sisters about her short-term dalliance with Logan, but the thought of sharing the news with her mom made her squirm.

How did you tell a parent that since Logan and she had buffed the kitchen countertop over a month ago, their time together had turned into one big session of marathon sex, or a bangaroo as Logan called it? Talk about a frickin' awkward conversation.

Not that she and Logan only had sex. To be fair, they talked a lot, cooked together, walked along the beach, and went out to dinner. She helped him with SAS, and he helped her train at her crappy gym. But before or after—and sometimes both before *and* after—any of those things happened, they usually tangled limbs, as Hannah would say. So far they'd done it on every surface in the cottage they felt confident would hold them, and a few they weren't so sure about.

Oh, hell. A stupid smile spread across her face from just thinking about him. All this time with Logan had dulled her sharp edges. Next thing she knew, she'd trade in her favorite black leather high-heeled boots for a pair of flowery ballet slippers. And even worse, all that sex was releasing so many feel-good hormones into her system, she couldn't work up a full head of steam, or even a little spark of irritation, about losing her edgy 'tude.

She climbed from the car and headed toward the house. Time to face the facts. Being with Logan made her happy—happier then she could ever remember being. All her joy-filled thoughts and blissful sighs of the past few weeks were wearing down her tough outer shell.

Grimacing, Kat thunked her palm against her forehead. *Joy-filled thoughts and blissful sighs?* Had she actually strung those frickin' words together in a sentence to describe herself?

"Shit." She had it bad.

She pushed open the side door and stepped into her parents' mudroom. About two point two seconds later, Cosmo charged through the doorway to greet her with a full-body wag and a giant stuffed giraffe clutched in his mouth.

"Hey, boy. Did you bring me a present?"

The moment she kneeled down to pat his head, he dropped to the floor and flopped onto his back—belly proudly displayed for her to scratch.

"Pulling the old bait-and-switch, huh?" She chuckled and gave his belly a few good rubs before climbing back to her feet. "Come on, boy. I'm already the last one here. We better join the party before Dad gives me another lecture on punctuality."

She walked through the spacious kitchen tricked out with the best of everything. She loved her parents—and it was none of her business—but they spent their money on the weirdest shit. Did a ten-thousand-dollar refrigerator keep food any colder than a thousand-dollar one? Nope. Sure, it looked prettier, but come on … Ten grand for a frickin' fridge?

Still shaking her head, she crossed the two-story great room that always smelled like lilacs, her mom's favorite scent, and spotted her parents and Claire out on the patio. Thankfully, the heat wave had passed, which meant they could be outside without the fear of melting into a puddle of sweat, and there was no prettier place to be outside than at her parents' place.

Set amid a forest of rolling hills on a secluded stretch of shore, the Bennett estate sat on the best piece of real estate within a hundred miles. Kat stepped onto the patio, the gentle breeze of the beautiful August evening rustling the leaves and swirling her hair around her shoulders.

"For the record, I'm not late." Grinning, she

tapped the time displayed on her mobile phone. "See? I've got two minutes to spare."

"Kat, dear, I'm so glad you could make it to dinner." Her mom placed her glass of Chardonnay on the large, extravagantly set patio table and pulled Kat in for a quick hug. "And I wouldn't care if you were late, as long as I can spend some time with you this evening."

Kat hugged her mom back. Ann Bennett was the only other Bennett woman who was as short and small-boned as her. Ann often joked the four Bennett kids lined up the same in age as they did in height. Pax being the tallest and oldest and Kat the shortest and youngest.

"Sounds like you miss having me around," Kat teased.

"Of course! Logan tells me you've been dedicating a lot of your time to helping him with the social outreach program." Her mom lowered her voice and glanced over Kat's shoulder. "I wish you would have brought him to dinner tonight. I want him to know we appreciate his help and enjoy having him in Silver Bay."

Kat enjoyed having him in Silver Bay too. She would enjoy having him anywhere, but that was probably not what her mom meant.

"Sorry, I forgot to ask him." Okay, that wasn't even close to true. She didn't want to invite him to a family dinner until some of the lust and—dammit—affection burnt out of her system, so she'd intentionally neglected to extend her mom's offer to Logan.

"It's nice of you to help, kiddo." Claire sauntered over with a sweet smile and overly interested look on her pretty face. "Everyone at Bennett is talking about the program. You guys have done a great job drumming up excitement." She took a sip of wine. "Considering he looks like an ad for surfboards and boardshorts, he's surprisingly efficient."

"Wow. You calling someone efficient is like me calling someone a badass. You must really like him."

Her sister shrugged. "He's sweet, funny, intelligent, and he works hard. What's not to like?"

"You forgot that he's hotter than sin," Kat teased.

"Kiddo, no woman he's ever met has forgotten that fact." Claire grinned. "So, what's it like living with him?"

"It's pretty ace."

"Ace?" her mom asked, looking confused.

"Great, excellent, cool. As an adjective, ace covers a lot of territory." Kat glanced around. "Where's everyone else?"

"Hannah took the kids for a walk along the shore before dinner." Her mom's face lit up at the thought of her two grandkids. "Grace loves to collect rocks, and Ty likes to see how far he can toss them into the lake." She turned toward Claire. "Honey, can you find them? Dinner will be ready soon."

"Sure, Mom," her sister said, glancing at the ever-present, multifunctional, guaranteed-to-keep-her-on-schedule watch strapped to her slender wrist. "I'm sure the kids are getting hungry."

Kat's heart squeezed as she watched Claire head toward the shore. While her divorced sis hadn't gotten lucky in love, she'd scored big in the kid department. Grace and nine-year-old Ty were pretty much the perfect niece and nephew in Kat's opinion.

"Do you think Paxton and Sage will decide to marry and have a baby soon?" Her mom stepped closer. "That would be absolutely wonderful. The first day I met Sage, I knew those two belonged together. I can't believe it took them so many years to figure it out themselves."

"Themselves?" Kat's dad gave a snort as he walked closer, wrapped an arm around his wife's shoulders, and raised an eyebrow. "The way I remember it, they had a little help."

Ann playfully jabbed her husband in the side with her elbow and looked around as if concerned about eavesdroppers on their very private estate. "Hush, Richard. I don't care how old my children get. If they need my help, I'm going to provide it."

Kat studied her mom through narrowed eyes. Ann Bennett was known for her grace and composure, but right now, she looked flustered. Clearing her throat, her mom smoothed down her already smooth hair, adjusted her already perfect dress, and looked everywhere except into Kat's eyes.

"Spill it, Mom."

Turning back, her mom tipped her chin up and leveled a determined look on her. "I have nothing to spill. And even if I did, everything worked out perfectly between Paxton and Sage, so it wouldn't matter anyway."

Kat chuckled and held up her hands in surrender. "Fine. Don't tell me what you did. Just don't go fooling around with my love life, okay?"

Her mom nibbled on her perfectly glossed lower lip, and her eyes widened just enough to send a twinge of unease through Kat. *Oh, frick.* What had her mom done to look so guilty?

Before she could press any further, Kat heard the door to the patio open and close behind her. Apparently, she wasn't the last to arrive for dinner. She turned around to see who'd joined them and jolted in surprise.

What the hell? Dressed in a pressed pair of black pants and pale blue shirt, John Vornado stood at the edge of the patio holding a bottle of wine.

"John, glad you accepted my offer." Her dad's voice boomed with pleasure. "I'm looking forward to hearing more about your help in getting Seniors Assisting Seniors off the ground.

"Thanks for the invitation." John smiled in greeting. "My part is very small compared to Logan and Kat. I'm just the liaison between the organization and the school."

Kat walked toward him. "I didn't know you'd be here." She planted a friendly kiss on his cheek and took the bottle from his hand. "Let me get you something to drink."

"A water would be fine."

"I suggest something stronger," she whispered with a conspiratorial wink.

A smile played around his lips as he considered her words. "All right. How about a beer?"

"Nice choice." She retrieved a beer for John and returned a moment later.

"Thanks," he said, looking down at her. "Your dad just mentioned that Logan is leaving town next month. I thought he'd be here longer."

She ignored the pressure in her chest and forced a smile. "Logan helped my brother start a similar community-based program in Costa Rica. He never intended to stay here more than a few months."

"So who is going to take over once he leaves?"

"Don't know." Kat glanced at her dad.

"Actually, dear," her dad said, looking suspiciously hopeful, "Logan thinks that you would be perfect for the job. He pointed out that you're smart, dedicated, and are so persuasive you could—" He compressed his lips and squinted, obviously trying to remember Logan's exact words—"sell a budgy smuggler to a wowser. Your mother and I have no idea what that means, but we're fairly certain it's a compliment." He shrugged. "Regardless, we agree with him about SAS."

"What the fu—"

"Katherine!" her mom interrupted with a stern look. "I know you enjoy colorful language, but this is neither the time nor place for it."

Wincing, Kat glanced her way. "Sorry, Mom. I got caught off guard." She turned back to her dad. "You want me to run SAS?"

"Yes. Logan's told us everything. He said you've met with multiple members of the community and that you're working on the logistics of creating a schedule of annual events to help the elderly—such as a multi-weekend leaf campaign in the fall to rake and bag leaves for the town's seniors. He also said you have some interesting ideas for fundraising and that you've already reached out to a handful of seniors who need help." He wrapped an arm around her and pulled her to his side. "Your mother and I had no idea you'd been helping Mrs. Dobolek. We're proud of you, and we'd like you to officially take over when Logan leaves."

"Why me?"

"Do you love helping others? Do you want to make SAS a success?"

"Yes and yes. But I've screwed up my life pretty good over the last year. Remember?"

Her mom stepped close and laid a hand on Kat's arm. "You quit your job, and it's taken you a while to find something that you love to do. That makes you human, dear, not a screwup. You should know, though, running a nonprofit organization takes a lot of work and offers little to no recognition in return."

Kat rolled her eyes. "You know I don't care about recognition."

"That's another reason why you're perfect for the job." Her dad dropped a kiss on the top of her head.

Oh shit. Kat could feel her nose swelling and her eyes filling. She blinked rapidly and swallowed down the lump forming in her throat. She was *so* not going to cry.

"One small problem," she said after getting her emotions under control. "I don't know how to run a nonprofit."

"We should ask Logan to stay longer to help smooth out the transition. He's such a nice young man." Her mom beamed encouragement at Kat. "I've already spoken to Celine. She said he's welcome to stay in the lake house until next summer and possibly even longer. She's happy to have someone trustworthy and responsible maintaining the home while they're not using it."

Kat's idiotic heart expanded like a balloon in her chest at the possibility of Logan staying longer.

"I'm sure that won't be necessary," her dad grumbled, bursting her idiotic heart balloon. "He's been here long enough. Besides," he said, turning to John, "one of the reasons I invited this young man to join us tonight was to ask for his continued help with SAS. As a lifetime resident of Silver Bay, John has valuable connections and an in-depth understanding of what makes our community special."

"Yes, dear, but John has a full-time job." Her mom's smile didn't even come close to reaching her eyes as she turned to face her husband. "Logan is able to dedicate more time to the program, and he has charmed everyone he's met. It's only a matter of time before he establishes firm ties to the community."

Kat's gaze ping-ponged between her parents. While her dad's expression had tightened with determination, her mom had assumed her stern I-know-I'm-right-and-I'm-not-backing-down stance. *What the frick?* If she didn't know better, she'd think her parents were trying to set her up with two different guys. But they weren't stupid enough to ...

Oh, shit. Kat resisted the urge to thunk her forehead with her palm. Who was she trying to kid? Of course, they were that stupid.

"Mom. Dad. Stop." She glared at each of them in turn. "I'm sure John is willing to continue helping with SAS. Right?" She cocked an eyebrow and looked at John, hating to put him on the spot, but this ridiculous conversation needed to end. Now.

John blinked twice, then offered a genuine smile. "I'm happy to help however I can."

"Excellent," her dad said, clapping him on the back.

"And I'm sure Logan will do the same," Kat

added dryly.

"Of course he will, dear. He's such a wonderful young man." Her mom smiled serenely at Kat. "Now let's enjoy some appetizers while we wait for Claire to fetch my beautiful grandchildren and Hannah."

Kat waited for her parents to walk toward the table covered with food before turning to John. "Sorry about that." She cringed. "I can help you slip out unnoticed if you want to make a run for it."

Restrained laughter tugged at John's lips and lit his dark-brown eyes. "I'll admit, the invitation to dinner came as a surprise. I haven't seen either of your parents in months. At least that mystery is solved."

"I'm with Logan," she said, keeping her voice low. "My parents don't know that, so I'd appreciate you not mentioning it. But I thought it might ease your mind to know that I'm not trying to get my hooks into you tonight."

"Your dad said Logan was leaving town next month."

"So what?"

"So he's a fool. If you looked at me the way you looked at him, I wouldn't be going anywhere."

"Uh ... uh," Kat stuttered. "John, I don't—"

"You don't have to say anything," he interrupted quietly. "You're with another guy right now, and I'm going to respect that. But once Logan leaves, you know where to find me."

Openmouthed, Kat stared at him until her father's voice broke through her hazy thoughts.

"John, if I remember correctly you love the water as much as I do. Would you like a tour of my boat before dinner?"

John turned toward her dad. "That would be great. Thanks, Mr. Bennett."

"Please, call me Richard."

Kat watched John head toward the dock at her father's side. She had to admit it felt nice knowing a good-looking, kind-hearted guy wanted to be with her for the long run.

Problem was, it was the wrong guy.

•••

A few hours past sunset that night, Kat jogged up the steps to the cottage feeling pretty darn good about herself. In the last month, she'd completed multiple sessions of self-defense training and worked out with Logan several times a week. She still felt uneasy alone at night, but at least she didn't flip out at the thought of it anymore. She might always have a scar, but the wound was healing.

"I'm home," she called out, walking into the cottage and spotting Logan lounging on the couch, wearing a pair of jeans and a thin gray T-shirt that stretched across his shoulders. "Miss me?"

Without saying a word, he stood up and walked straight toward her, his gaze heated and locked on hers. She sucked in a breath, and her heart kicked up a notch. The man truly was sex walking.

He pulled her close, slid a hand under her shirt, and captured her mouth in a kiss full of tongue and delicious intent. He lifted his head from hers a few minutes later, leaving her breathless and achy with need.

"Yeah, tiger. I missed you." His voice rumbled

through her, sending off a shiver of desire. He slipped her shirt over her head and then pushed her skirt off her hips to the floor. Her bra and his clothes quickly followed.

"I've been home for five minutes, and you've already stripped me down to my panties and heels."

"No worries." Lifting her hair away, he kissed her neck and caressed her hip with his free hand. "I'll let you leave the heels on."

His smile promised wicked pleasure. He lifted her into his arms, carried her to his bedroom, and set her on her feet so she faced the waist-high dresser with a mirror hung above it. He grabbed the edge of the dresser, one arm locked on each side of her. Pressing his chest against her back, he pinned her to the dresser and continued to nuzzle her neck.

Needing to touch him, Kat tried to turn around, but he dropped his hands to her hips and held her in place.

"I want you to see how hot we are together," he murmured inches from her ear.

Mesmerized by his silky voice and wicked tongue, Kat braced her hands on the dresser, and locked her gaze on the mirror and the man reflected behind her. A slow, sexy smile lifted the corners of his mouth as he cupped a breast with one hand and sent the other on a southerly exploration.

"Taking a trip Down Under, ay?" She grinned, tipping her head to the side.

She felt him chuckle behind her. "Too right, darl."

Her grin slipped and she sucked in a breath as she watched him toy with her nipple, pinching and tweaking the hardened peak, and then gliding his palm across her skin to deliver the same treatment to her other aching nipple. Every touch, every tease, shot off an electrified bolt of desire between her legs.

"You're so bloody beautiful it hurts when I'm not touching you," Logan said, his other hand sliding farther down her belly.

Her head fell back to his chest and her breathing grew heavier, but her gaze stayed locked on the mirror as his hand slipped into her black lace panties.

She cried out and jerked against him when he circled her leisurely with his finger. She closed her eyes, focusing on his touch.

He stilled behind her, and both of his hands left her body. "Look at me, darl."

She forced her eyes open, finding his in the mirror.

"There's my tiger." He lowered his mouth and licked, kissed, and sucked her neck as his fingers resumed their delicious torment.

She locked her arms on the dresser and rose to her tiptoes. Her legs went rigid as she ground against his hand, desperate for release. "Don't stop."

He bit the sensitive spot below the corner of her jaw and rolled a nipple between his thumb and index finger. Then, with his other hand, he pushed two fingers into her.

"Don't stop," she cried again, throwing her head back, eyes closed, seeking release.

His hand buried deep inside of her went still. She moaned and squirmed, but his fingers didn't move.

"Please, tiger. I want you to see how beautiful you are when you come for me."

Kat opened her eyes and looked again to the mirror. Logan's tanned arms were crossed in front of her pale skin, holding her to his muscular body as he teased her.

"I want you to remember how good I make your body feel." He gave her a sexy, sinful smile and crooked the fingers in her to rub the sensitive spot deep inside. When her knees buckled, he tightened his arms around her to hold her up. He continued to circle the spot until she was breathless and begging in his arms.

When he slipped his fingers from inside her and circled the swollen bundle of nerves between her thighs, she nearly went over the edge. But he stopped moments before she fell, thrust his fingers back into her, and started the cycle over. Her gaze on the mirror, Kat thrashed wildly in his arms as he continued thrusting, rubbing, and circling.

"Come for me, tiger," he murmured, circling demanding fingers over her swollen flesh.

She exploded in his arms. Light flashed in her eyes as waves of mind-blowing pleasure washed through her.

One hour and another orgasm later, Kat lay snuggled against Logan, her head resting on his chest. Nearly comatose, Logan was flat on his back, eyes closed and breathing deeply—the hand gently toying with her hair was the only sign he hadn't passed out after their latest round of sex.

Logan's heartbeat under her made her feel oddly content until she remembered how little time she had left with him. What chance did she have of ever finding someone like him again? While no statistician, Kat figured those odds to be somewhere between shitty and impossible. What if her summer fling turned out to be the mother of all frickin' backfires and ruined her for all other men?

"What's wrong, tiger?" Logan's low, sleepy voice rumbled under her.

"What makes you think something's wrong?" she asked, attempting a deflection.

She felt him shrug a shoulder. "I know you."

Sitting up, she pulled her legs under her. His gaze immediately locked on her naked breasts. With a dramatic eye roll, she snatched a blue T-shirt from the floor and slipped it on over her head. "Do I have your full attention now?"

"Darl, you had my full attention before," he drawled.

"You mean my breasts had your attention."

He gave her a wicked grin. "Okay, fine. Now I'm focused. What's up?"

"I kinda realized that maybe there's a small chance that you and your ridiculously talented abilities could have possibly set the bar too high to reach for any other guy that I might—you know—someday meet."

Logan studied her for a long beat, his eyebrows furrowed in confusion. "Was that English?"

Kat jumped to her feet and paced the room. She had to keep this about sex. He liked relationships simple, and she'd promised him no strings. She couldn't renege now. "Pay attention! I'm afraid I'll never find anyone as good at sex as you are!" she yelled, damn well keeping silent about the part where she'd never find anyone she liked as well as him either.

"Good." He sat up in the bed and laced his hands behind his head, looking smug and sexy at the same time.

"Good?" She narrowed her eyes.

"I don't want you having sex with anyone else. Good, bad, or otherwise."

"You're leaving next month." Kat hated to point out the obvious, but it seemed he needed a reality check.

Climbing from bed, Logan shook his head and walked toward his dresser. After pulling on a pair of boxer briefs, he turned back to face her. "Doesn't matter," he said running a hand through his messy hair. "Still don't want you with another guy."

She opened her mouth to give him some sort of flippant retort when the truth suddenly pierced her heart and deflated her anger. How could she argue when she frickin' agreed with him?

"And I don't want you having sex with another woman," she snapped. In fact, the thought of him with someone else simultaneously dropped her stomach and raised her blood pressure. "So where does that leave us?"

Shaking his head, he blew out a long, slow breath. "No idea."

"This wasn't supposed to happen." Talking more to herself than Logan, Kat began pacing the room. "Crashing with you for the summer was supposed to be a fun memory for both of us, not a life changer."

As she paced by him, Logan wrapped his hand around her arm and drew her to a stop. "I've changed your life?"

"I don't know. Maybe." She dropped her forehead into the heel of her hand and rubbed hard, hoping that might somehow clear away her confusion. "I know that when my dad tried to hook me up with John tonight, I wasn't interested."

Logan's grip tightened on her arm. "John was at dinner?"

"Yeah. My dad invited him. Obvious attempt at matchmaking, but all I could think about was you."

"Your dad fucking invited him?"

Kat's attention jolted to Logan. He stood stone-still in front of her, jaw locked and eyes raging with anger. She'd never seen him so ticked off. Actually, she'd never seen *anyone* so ticked off.

"He tells me to keep my hands off and then invites another guy to have a go at you, ay? Guess I'm not good enough." Scowling, Logan dropped her arm.

"It's not like that," she said, placing her palm on his chest. "Dad knows you're leaving next month. He doesn't want me to get hurt, that's all."

"No need to make excuses for him. I'm used to it."

"What are you used to?"

He clamped his mouth shut, and his body stiffened beneath her hand. His stubborn expression communicated that he'd rather eat a boot than talk to her, but she didn't back down.

"Logan, did my dad do something else to piss you off?"

"Not yours."

"Who then?" she pressed.

"I don't have a good history with parents. Seems I'm not who they want their little girls to grow old with." Logan gave a bitter smile. "Face it, Kat, I'm good for fun but not for the future."

The pain in his voice and the bleakness in his eyes made her want to rip apart whatever asshole had torn Logan down in the past. "Whoever said that is full of shit. You're amazing." She tapped her fingertip hard against his chest. "You've got a great heart. Anyone would be lucky to have you in their future."

He snorted. Whether in agreement or disgust, she wasn't quite sure, but his expression was a little less ready-to-rampage than a second ago. She took that as a good sign.

She slid her arms around him and hugged him tightly. "You told me once that you can't let the assholes of the world stop you from living."

"Yeah. So?"

"So maybe it's time you take your own advice."

Logan didn't react for a long beat, and then he gave a full-bodied sigh and wrapped his arms around her and dropped a kiss on her head. "We should get some sleep."

They climbed back into bed, and she snuggled against his side. A short time later, Kat felt his body relax and his breathing settle into a peaceful rhythm.

Sleep didn't come so easy for her. She couldn't stop thinking about their conversation. She'd always assumed Logan's commitment-free take on relationships made him happy. Now, she couldn't help but wonder if he also used it as a defense mechanism.

And then she wondered how else his past had affected him. And then she wondered why the hell she was lying awake thinking like a frickin' shrink. And then she was pissed at herself.

As she finally slipped into a restless sleep, one last thought grated through her mind.

When had her let's-make-fun-memories-together-and-then-go-our-separate-ways summer fling turned into a staying-up-all-night-for-all-the-wrong-reasons relationship?

So much for keeping things simple.

TWELVE

KAT sighed in relief as the last of the morning crowd cleared out of Fresh. Plunking into a chair, she rested her head on the cool wood table in front of her and closed her eyes. Her limbs went slack, her mind drifting into that hazy zone between consciousness and sleep.

It had been two weeks since her parents asked her to run SAS at the family dinner, and in another two weeks, she would be taking over the non-profit, moving into her own apartment, and Logan would be gone. The thought of him leaving hurt like crazy. She hadn't a clue how or when she'd ever get over him.

She'd even toyed with the idea of asking him to stay longer. Then they'd spent a day apartment hunting for her. While she'd been grouchy about finding a new place to live, Logan had been focused and insistent on her choosing an apartment—as if he couldn't frickin' wait for her to move out so he could move on.

On top of everything else, she'd never been so tired in her life. Exhaustion was too mild a word for the near comatose condition she'd been fighting off the past few days. Her limited hours of sleep were hitting her harder than expected.

"You still among the living?" Hannah asked, stepping out of the back room.

Kat groaned in response.

"I saw you drink at least four cups of coffee today. How can you possibly be that tired? Have you been working late on SAS? Or is it your extracurricular activities with Mr. Hunky Roommate that's keeping you up all night?"

Kat didn't answer. After hours of work, they were finally alone in the café. If her sister would only stop chattering—or earbashing as Logan would say—she could get some sleep and maybe shake off this bone-weary fatigue.

Seconds from drifting off, she jolted at the sound of a chair sliding up next to her.

Kat squinted at her sister. "Do you have to be so loud? I need sleep."

"Honey, the way you look, you need a doctor. What's wrong with you?"

"Tired." She settled her head back on the table. "Really tired."

"Come on, you need a bed more than I need help in the café." Hannah pulled Kat to her feet, then gave her a gentle nudge toward the stairs leading to her apartment. "Go take a nap before you pass out."

"I'll take you up on the nap, but just to be clear," Kat said, taking off her apron, "I'm not the type of girl to pass out." Then she took a step forward, and damn if her head didn't spin like a cheap-ass carnival ride. She stumbled to a stop and grabbed the back of the chair to catch her balance. Her breaths came short and choppy as she fought the blackness creeping into the corners of her vision. Holy hell, she might actually faint.

"I gotcha." Hannah wrapped an arm around her and pulled her against her side for support. "You need to sit down."

"Not here. Too many eyes." Kat nodded to the wall of windows.

"Fine. Let's get you upstairs."

Too focused on staying upright to form actual words, Kat nodded in agreement and let her sister lead her up the stairs and into the apartment.

Kat dropped onto Hannah's overstuffed couch, propped her elbows on her knees, and held her spinning head in her hands. "Damn, I feel nauseous and light-headed. I must have overdone the caffeine." She looked up at Hannah. "You should post a warning on that stuff."

"I'm not sure it's the caffeine." Hannah's concerned tone and stunned expression sent a jolt of anxiety straight to Kat's already shaky gut. "Remember when Claire almost blacked out at the family dinner about ten years ago?"

"Yeah. Why? You saying it's something hereditary?"

"Kinda." Hannah cringed, her expression a mix of reluctance and apology. "Claire was early in her pregnancy with Ty. Mom told her not to worry too much about it because the same dizziness happened to her with each of her pregnancies."

Kat's head shot up, and she sucked in air.

Warning bells and adrenaline escalated her to high-alert status in two seconds flat. "What the hell are you saying?"

"Is there any chance you're pregnant?"

Kat shook her head in frantic denial. "We *always* use a condom."

"No birth control is one hundred percent reliable. When was your last period?"

Oh. Holy. Shit. Kat jumped to her feet and started pacing circles around the room. "It's irregular. I don't keep track." She threw her hands up for emphasis as her mind worked through the possibility of an unexpected pregnancy.

A baby. Could she actually be carrying Logan's baby? She pressed her palm to her flat stomach. Her heart hammered in her chest, her fingers shook, and her breathing approached hyperventilating levels.

Hannah grabbed her arm and dragged her back to the couch. "Sit down and let's think about this. We don't know anything for sure yet."

Kat dropped into the seat. Pregnant. How could that happen? Okay, she knew *how* it happened but still couldn't believe it might have happened to her.

"No matter what, it's going to be okay." Hannah crouched in front of her and gripped her hands. "You don't even know if you're pregnant, so there's no need to panic. You stay here and try to relax. I'll lock up the café and drive around until I find a convenience-store clerk who doesn't know me and buy a pregnancy test. I'll get back here as quick as I can. Okay?"

Kat nodded. Hannah was right. She needed to know for sure.

Her sister pulled her in for a quick hug. "It's

going to be okay," she repeated, then grabbed her purse and bolted out of the apartment.

Kat hugged her knees to her chest as a kaleidoscope of scenarios whirled through her mind. How would Logan react to an accidental pregnancy? Would he stick around? Stay in Silver Bay to be with his child? With her? What if he thought she got pregnant on purpose to trap him? Would he propose because it was the right thing to do? And if he did propose, would she accept knowing he'd only done it for the baby?

One thing she knew for sure, when the dust settled, Logan would make a great dad. He was kind, funny, generous, and truly cared about others. He might look like sex walking, but there was so much more to him. No matter what happened between them, he'd be there for his child.

The image of him holding a tiny baby in his big hands flashed through her mind. Her heart swelled to bursting and pounded in her chest as realization slammed into her.

She loved him. Baby or no baby … she loved him.

Un-frickin'-believable. She'd fallen for Logan even though he didn't do love.

Kat's head spun and her vision blurred. She frantically gulped in air and tried to slow her heartbeat before she passed out. Life-changing revelations could do a number on the nervous system.

Finally, she heard Hannah open the door to the café downstairs. A moment later, her sister jogged up the steps with a triumphant smile. "I got one." She held up a small white paper bag. "It took me three stops, but I finally found a pierced-up teenager working behind a counter. The kid didn't know or care who I was or what I was buying. We're in the clear."

Kat gave her a weak grin. "Thanks. The last thing I need is word getting back to Dad." She boosted herself off the couch. "Here goes everything."

In less time than it took her to brush her teeth, Kat took the test. She paced the small bathroom waiting for the result. Whether it turned out to be positive or negative, she knew her life had already changed.

She'd finally admitted to herself that she loved Logan and wanted him to stay with her—baby or no baby—forever.

The timer on her phone beeped at the two-minute mark. Holding her breath and heart pounding in her throat, she wrapped her arms around herself and leaned over the counter to read the results.

The bright green plus sign dropped her stomach to her toes. She took two steps back, bumped against the wall, and slowly slid to the floor.

She loved Logan.

She was carrying his baby in her belly.

And she didn't want a half-assed, water-downed version of a family where they lived separate lives while raising a child together—she wanted a fairy-tale ending.

She tipped her head against the cold tile wall and rolled her eyes at her own idiocy.

Unbelievable.

She'd turned into a lovesick fool desperate for a

frickin' happily-ever-after with a guy who was leaving town in two weeks. And even though her gut told her Logan would either stay in Silver Bay or return to town frequently once he found out about the baby, she wanted more.

She wanted him to stick with her—not because of the baby, but because he loved her.

Kat pushed herself to her feet as a bare-bones plan took shape in her mind. She stepped out of the bathroom and gave her worried looking sis a weak smile.

"It's positive."

"Oh, Kat." Hannah's face scrunched with concern as she stepped toward Kat, arms outstretched.

"It's okay." Kat held up her hand to stop her advance. "I haven't totally freaked out yet, and I'd like to keep it that way. So let's dial down the emotion. And speaking of overly emotional, you've gotta promise me you won't tell anyone. Not Claire. Not Mom. Not Sage. Not anyone."

"Are you keeping the baby?"

Not entirely sure her voice would hold, Kat nodded in confirmation.

"Then they're going to find out." Hannah's voice raised in volume as she slowly enunciated each word.

"Yeah, but I can't tell them if I'm not telling Logan."

Her sister's eyes went wide. "You're not telling Logan you're pregnant? Bad idea, Kat." Hannah shook her head rapidly, her dark ponytail emphasizing her words as it whipped from side to side. "You *have* to tell him."

"Chill out. I have a plan," Kat said, sounding a

lot more confident than she felt.

"You're going to need one hell of a plan to justify keeping the father of your child in the dark." Hannah followed her to the small kitchen at the far end of the room.

Kat scooped up a handful of almonds from a hand-painted bowl on the countertop. "You're supposed to fall in love, commit to one another, and then make a baby, right? Well, Logan and I kinda skipped the first two steps and jumped straight to the third. I think I can pull it all back on track, but I can't tell him I'm pregnant yet." She popped the nuts into her mouth and started munching.

"This plan of yours is making my eyelid twitch." Hannah pressed two fingertips to her closed eye. "Just to be clear, that is so *not* a good sign."

"I love him." Kat shrugged, "And I have to know if he wants me in his life *before* he finds out he's stuck with me there."

"Oh, Kat. I'm a realist, and this sounds like a really, really bad idea. Please just tell him about the baby."

Kat thought about it a beat. "I will tell him. Soon. But not before I find out if he's willing to stay in Silver Bay to be with me. Just me."

"Fine." Hannah blew out an exasperated breath. "Then please tell me how you plan to figure that out before you almost pass out again or barf on him?"

"Easy." Kat drew in a long breath and tipped her head from side-to-side, trying to ease the tension already tightening her neck and shoulders. "I'll ask him. Tonight."

Hannah blinked. "What are you going to say? 'Logan, I know you're leaving the country soon, but

I was wondering if you'd rather give up your carefree life of adventure and excitement to grow old with me instead?' "

"Well, jeez, I'll phrase it better than that," Kat grumbled.

Hannah cocked an eyebrow.

"I'll be persuasive … you know, point out some of my more endearing qualities."

"Will that be enough for him to stay?"

"Only one way to find out." Kat tipped up her chin, squared her tense shoulders, and headed for the door.

•••

Logan turned onto the lane leading to the cottage. He had two weeks left in Silver Bay and only twelve nights left sharing the cottage with Kat. His hands tightened on the wheel. He didn't want to leave Silver Bay, and he sure as hell didn't want to leave Kat. But their relationship had never been meant for the long haul.

Forcing himself to relax his hands, he pulled to a stop, scooped up the wildflowers he'd picked on the way home, and climbed from the car. In thirteen days, the lease started on Kat's new place. They'd found her a small apartment in a secure building near the town's college that even had a security service to monitor the parking lot and entranceway via cameras. Kat said she'd be fine living there alone, but he still was worried about her.

He hated to think she'd have no one to turn to once he left Silver Bay. He'd tried to convince her to tell her family about the mugging. In typically Kat fashion, she'd refused, claiming she didn't need their help. Turned out his Kat didn't need help with much of anything. He'd been filling her in on his experience with the best way to launch and manage SAS, but she was already well equipped to hit the ground running when she started full-time next week.

He entered the cottage and scanned the area, his pulse kicking up at the thought of seeing her. While lively music filled the room and a trio of tiered candles burned atop the coffee table, he didn't see Kat anywhere. The delicious smell of warm balsamic vinegar mixed with olive oil and basil coming from the oven, however, meant she was cooking one of his favorite chicken dishes for dinner and couldn't be too far away.

When he stepped farther into the room and heard the shower running, he hustled into the kitchen. He should have enough time to put the flowers in water before she returned to the cozy scene he'd come home to.

Huh. Home? It'd been a long time since anywhere he lived had felt like home. And while the cottage was great, he knew Kat was the real reason he loved living there. *Shit.* He shook his head, trying to push away the thought. Like a complete fuck-up, he'd fallen for Kat. Leaving her might bloody well kill him, but he didn't have a choice. He'd learned the hard way—no woman wanted to spend forever with a bloke who had no fucking future to speak of.

The only way he'd survive was by leaving before she came to her bloody senses and kicked his arse out. It wouldn't take a smart lady like Kat long to realize how little he had to offer her. Soon she would want more from him than fantastic sex, and except for keeping her safe at night, he had nothing else to give her.

She'd been upfront from the beginning. She'd only wanted him for great sex and fun memories. He'd done everything in his power to give her both. Hopefully that would be enough for her to remember him.

He'd damn well never forget her.

•••

Kat decided a walk along the beach after making Logan his favorite dinner would be the best time to pop her doozy of a question. So here they were, walking along the shore, hand in hand, enjoying a beautiful late-August sunset together. The warm breeze rolled melodic waves onto the sand and swirled her long hair around her shoulders. It was all very romantic. Or it would be if she didn't feel like she could puke at any moment.

She was so nervous she couldn't think straight. It had only been a few hours since the tiny green plus sign announced the very big change coming in her future. While the possibility of Logan sharing that future with her made her heart swell with a bunch of sappy emotions, the knowledge that asking Logan to stay might send him running for the hills did a swell job holding her enthusiasm in check.

Damn. How'd guys do this? It took a hell of a lot more bravery to put herself on the line than she'd ever realized. Kat felt ready to hyperventilate, and all she planned to do was ease Logan into the idea of sticking around longer, fearing that asking for any bigger commitment at this point could scare him away for good.

Hopefully, when she asked him to stay, he'd say yes. And if not? She shook that anxiety-raising thought from her head. No need to stress out about him ditching her until it actually happened. She'd cross that crappy-ass bridge when and if she ever got to it.

"Pax called today. Sounds like he and Sage had an ace time hiking to Machu Picchu."

"Huh?" Kat mumbled, barely able to hear Logan over the pounding sound of her own heartbeat.

"Your brother and Sage are back in Costa Rica from their trip to Peru, ay."

"Oh."

She could feel Logan laughing as he slung an arm around her shoulder, hugged her into his side, and kissed the top of her head. "You're the one who suggested we take a walk, but your mind is somewhere far away."

Ugh. He was right. She needed to man up. Slipping from his embrace, Kat took a step away from the warmth of his solid body, tipped her chin up, and waited for him to meet her gaze.

He turned to look at her, his handsome face marred with unease. "What's going on, tiger?"

"Moment of truth." She tipped her head from side to side to work out some of the tension, then locked her gaze on his. "I lied to you." She shoved her fisted hands into the pockets of her stretchy skirt. "I said that the summer would be enough. But it's not. I'd like you to stay longer." She sucked in a quick breath. "I'm not ready for you to leave."

A muscle jumped in Logan's jaw. "How much

longer you reckon until you *are* ready for me to leave? A month? Maybe two?"

Kat reared back, surprised by his hard tone. "That's not what I meant."

"Would you rather just let me know when you're tired of me so I can take off then?"

"No." Kat shook her head. "Of course not." She couldn't make sense of the intense waves of emotion radiating off of Logan's rigid body.

What the hell? Kat's rising frustration did an ace job clearing away her confusion. She stepped forward and poked him in the chest. "Don't put words in my mouth. I never said I'd get tired of you, jerkface. I was trying to tell you that I like you more than a little bit. In fact, I like you more than a lot of bits." Kat crossed her arms over her chest and glared up at the big idiot. "I don't want you to move. I like living with you."

As the last of the day's light slipped beneath the horizon, the emotion drained from Logan in one massive, full-bodied sigh. "I'm sorry, darl. I misunderstood. If you need me to live with you, I can stay a little longer."

"Need?" Kat stammered the question, simultaneously shocked and ticked off.

Screw that. She didn't *need* anyone.

"I know you're scared to be alone. But—"

"Are you serious?" She swallowed to clear the lump forming in her throat and hoped like hell the darkness masked the pain his words had shot through her. "Do you think I'm so weak and pathetic that I need a guy to take care of me? What? Did you think you owe it to Pax to babysit his fraidy-cat little sister?"

"No. It's not like that." He scrubbed a hand down his face. "I wouldn't do it for Pax. I want to help you."

"Shit. So I'm a charity case to you?" Kat asked, swiping away a frickin' tear. "Is the sex an added perk, or did you do that out of pity too?"

His mouth twisted into a grimace. "Christ, Kat, nothing is out of pity. You know I ... care about you," he said, his voice low and raw.

When he lifted his hand to reach for her, she took a step back and locked her arms across her body. "But not enough for you to want to stay longer."

His outstretched arm dropped to his side with a dejected thud. He drew in a tense breath and his expression hardened. "You said it yourself. I don't stick." He shook his head. "It's better that way."

She sniffed in a quick breath and faked a smile. "Good news. You're off the hook. I'm not afraid to be alone anymore. Haven't been for a while. So there's no need for you to stick with me." Shooting for careless indifference, she shrugged a shoulder. "In fact, now that I know the truth, big guy, I'd prefer to be alone."

Logan opened his mouth to say something, then slowly closed it and nodded his head in easy acceptance of her words. "I'll go." He shoved his hands into the pockets of his jeans, turned away, then paused—his black silhouette blocked the faint light from the distant cottage.

"It's dark. Do you need me to walk you back?" He didn't bother looking at her when he asked the question. Not that it mattered. The flat tone of his voice made it clear he was offering out of duty rather than the desire to be with her.

"No, Logan. I don't need you for anything."

He dipped his head in silent acknowledgment, his broad shoulders straightening a fraction, like a frickin' weight had just been lifted from them. "Goodbye, tiger," he murmured. The words sounded more like an afterthought than the deathblow to her dreams that they were.

His farewell hit her harder than a fist. After he walked away and disappeared in the darkness, she wanted to drop to her knees. Fighting back the sobs building in her chest, she clenched her eyes closed and locked her arms tight around her body in a desperate attempt to stop the gut wrenching pain from ripping her apart. She couldn't fall apart. She had someone depending on her now.

Kat gritted her teeth, sucked in air, and slipped a hand to her still-flat stomach. No matter what happened, she had to be strong. And even though the pain snaking around her heart constricted it so ruthlessly she could barely breathe, she wouldn't beg Logan to stay, and she sure as hell wouldn't use the baby to guilt him into it.

She'd wanted an answer, and she'd gotten one.

She wasn't enough to make Logan stick.

THIRTEEN

"OH, Kat. You have to tell him. You have to, have to, have to tell him." Even lecturing from over two thousand miles away, Sage's pleading tone came through Kat's cell phone loud and clear. "You just *have* to tell him."

Kat rolled her eyes and took a big bite of the juicy red apple she'd picked at the orchard outside of town yesterday. Sage had been her best friend since college, and while she meant well, Kat wasn't in the mood to talk about Logan. "I'm not sure I understand what you're trying to tell me. Do you think I should tell him or not?" she asked dryly, munching away.

"Don't be a smart aleck. Logan deserves to know you're carrying his child. And I don't think I can hold Pax off much longer. Since he found out you're pregnant, he's been threatening to hunt Logan down and ... Well, there's no need to repeat that kind of language. Frankly, I'm thankful Logan didn't return to Costa Rica after leaving Silver Bay. Pax is going to need a lot more time to cool off before he sees him again."

Kat puffed out a sigh and tossed the remains of her apple into the open trash bin across the cottage's kitchen from where she sat. Her friend sure knew how to ruin a beautiful fall day. "Tell my big brother to stay out of it. This whole thing is my responsibility. I can handle it by myself."

It'd been well over a month since Logan left town. The leaves had started to change colors, and her stomach had rounded into a small baby bump. While her family and Sage knew about the pregnancy, she hadn't felt the need to share the info with anyone else yet.

After the jerkface had left her alone and crying on the beach, Kat had returned to the cottage to find it empty. In less than an hour, Logan had disappeared from her life. When she'd finally stopped crying, roughly a week later, she'd put on her big girl panties and pieced together a plan to get through the next few years. She canceled the lease on the apartment she'd planned to move to. Thankfully, her mom's friend Celine had happily agreed to let her pay rent to stay at the cottage until she found a house to buy. Kat wanted her kid to grow up with a front porch, a yard, and maybe even a dog someday. She didn't need anything fancy, which worked out great because her savings account couldn't afford fancy anyway.

She'd left the café and started working full-time at SAS. Well, almost full-time. She still slipped away two afternoons a week to help Mrs. D., Lillian, Margaret, and Harry.

As long as she ignored the fact that the guy she

loved had ditched both her and the unborn child she
hadn't figured out how to tell him about, things were
going fine. Of course, it was damn hard to ignore
that fact when her bestie kept badgering her about
telling said idiot about the pregnancy.

"You wouldn't have to handle it by yourself if
you would just tell Logan you're carrying his baby.
And stop rolling your eyes at me. You know I'm
right."

"Jeez, I'm not rolling my eyes," Kat lied, rolling
her eyes again. "And I am going to tell him. I'm just
taking my time. I wanna, you know"— she clicked
her tongue—"do it right. Problem is, I haven't been
able to find a line of 'Guess-what! You knocked me
up!' greeting cards." She shrugged. "I'm going to
look on Amazon later. They carry everything."

"That's it. I'm flying to Silver Bay tomorrow."
Sage's voice rang with a scary level of determination.
"It kills me to hear you trying to hide your pain
behind sarcasm and jokes. I'll catch the morning
flight and be there by tomorrow night. We'll figure
this out together."

"Chill out. I left Logan a voicemail a few weeks
ago saying I needed to talk to him. I'll tell him about
the baby whenever he bothers to call me back." Kat
tightened her grip on her phone and started
nervously tapping her fingers on one of the
numerous parenting books scattered on the kitchen
island. "I know you want to help, and I love you for
it, but if you rushed here every time I said something
sarcastic, you'd have to catch a flight north every
other day. Maybe more. I really am okay. Or I will be
someday. I think," she added lamely.

"Do you love him?"

Kat thought about it a beat before answering. "Yeah. I love him."

"Does he know that?"

"Doesn't matter. He left when I asked him to stay."

"If he knew—"

"The last thing I want is for him to stay with me out of pity or obligation." Frustration and pride shook her words but strengthened her resolve.

"But—"

"Discussion closed. Now please stop worrying about me and go back to whatever you were doing before you called." Eager to change the subject, Kat rushed on, knowing exactly how to disorient her overly proper friend. "What were you and my brother up to today? Another round of Captain Pax and his Saucy Wench?"

Sage let out a choked gasp.

Kat grimaced. "Oh my God, you were!" *Eww. Major backfire!* A shiver of grossness ran down her spine. "Why would you tell me that?"

"I didn't tell you. You guessed. Besides we didn't even do that today."

"Yeah, but now I know you *have* done it." Kat pounded her forehead with the heel of her hand. "I'll never be able to forget that visual."

"I've traumatized you," Sage teased, her tone rich with amusement. "Now I'm definitely flying back to help."

"Appreciated but not needed. Save the visit for after the kiddo is born. I've been reading some books on babies, and there's some seriously scary shit in there. Did you know they eat and poop every seven and a half minutes and only sleep for half an hour at a time until they're like four years old?"

"That can't possibly be true."

"My numbers may be a bit off." Kat dismissed Sage's skepticism with a flick of her wrist and started pacing nervous laps around the living room and kitchen. "But you get my point. Plus, there are a shit-ton of experts preaching theories on how to raise a kid and nobody can agree on which one is right. The only frickin' thing they agree on is if you do it wrong, you'll screw the kid up for life."

"You're not going to screw your kid up," Sage said matter-of-factly.

"Yeah, right," Kat groused. "Did you know I'm not supposed to swear around the kid? And when did 'stupid' become a cuss word? I let that little beauty fly in the grocery store line a week ago, and some woman covered her kid's ears, nailed me with the stink-eye, and said she doesn't use *that* word in front of children." She scrunched her eyes closed and collapsed onto the couch, her emotions downshifting in one giant hormonal swing. "I'm going to be a horrible mother."

"You're going to be a wonderful mom."

"How can you say that?" Her voice shook and eyes filled with tears. Frickin' out-of-control emotions. "And I'm not being sarcastic this time. I really, really want a reason to believe you."

"Because you're a wonderful friend, sister, and daughter. Becoming an amazing mother will be a natural transition for you."

"I guess my total awesomeness went unnoticed by Logan."

"It's his loss, the jerkface," Sage declared firmly as only a best friend could.

Kat snorted. The huge piece of her heart that Logan had ripped out and taken with him sure as hell felt like her loss. Yes, she would have her baby, her home, her job, her friends, and her family. And she loved them all, but without Logan her life would never be full.

"I gotta go. Tell everyone at La Vida I said hey, and I'll call you soon." She disconnected before the tears slipping down her cheeks turned into an all-out cryfest.

For the millionth time, she wondered what Logan was doing right now. She knew he wasn't in Costa Rica or Silver Bay, which left pretty much anywhere else in the world as a possibility. Did he miss her or had she already been replaced? Did he even think about her? What if he'd deep-sixed thoughts of her like all his other easily forgotten romantic liaisons?

The idea compressed what was left of her heart into a tight, painful knot. She ground the heel of her hand into her aching chest. As much as she hated the thought of Logan forgetting her, she hated the thought of being his latest and greatest mistake even more. And she knew once he got around to calling her back and she filled him in on his impending fatherhood, he'd never be able to forget her—even if he wished he could.

•••

The fist slammed into Logan's face with bone-crunching effectiveness, snapping his head back and igniting a blaze of lights behind his eyelids. He stumbled back to stop from landing on his arse.

Damn. He'd forgotten how hard Pax could punch.

Logan wiped the back of his hand across the spew of blood coming from his mouth. "Hey, mate. Good to see you too."

Pax shoved past him, charged into the shitty Chicago flat, and scanned the small room with a sneer. "So this is what you left my sister for?" He jerked his arm toward the only stuff in the place—a threadbare chair, a beat-up table, and a saggy mattress shoved into the corner. "Three months. You walked away from her three months ago, and this is all you have to show for it? What the hell is wrong with you?"

Logan swiped more blood from his lips and shrugged.

Glaring, Pax shook his head with disappointment and rage burning in his eyes. "This life of yours ... never letting anyone close, never building a future, never giving a fuck about anything for long. Is that really who you are? Because, honest to God, I thought you were better than that."

"Nice speech, but you're wasting your breath." Logan dropped into the sole chair in the room and stretched his legs out in front of him. "I'm surprised to see you." He figured Pax would be thrilled to have a bloke like him out of his sister's life.

"It took a large check to a PI after you changed your phone number, but I wasn't giving up until I had the chance to tell you what an enormous fuck-up you are in person," Pax growled. "And I wanted to slam my fist into that pretty-boy face of yours." He flexed his right hand like he was making sure it still worked in case he decided to punch him again.

"It was worth every damn penny, by the way."

Logan rubbed his jaw and gave a mirthless chuckle. "Glad you enjoyed it, mate. Maybe someday you'll learn to hit hard enough to actually do some damage."

"If you don't get your ass to Silver Bay and beg Kat to take you back, I'll do a hell of a lot more damage. Goddammit, Logan, it's almost Christmas. Do you want Kat spending it alone and—" Paxton abruptly snapped his mouth closed, his jaw tightening. He drew in a deep breath before repeating, "Do you want her spending it alone?"

Logan snorted. "I take it Kat didn't tell you anything about our last conversation because she made it clear she preferred being alone."

"She didn't tell me anything," Pax snarled. "I should fucking kill you for using my sister for sex. Was she just another easy lay to you?"

Logan shot to his feet and charged toward Pax. He had a couple inches on the bastard and would happily use that advantage to beat the shit out of him. He stopped less than a foot away from Pax, pissed off and ready to fight. "Watch your fucking mouth, mate, or I'm going start hitting back."

Pax stilled, confusion then surprise flashing across his features. "Holy shit. You love her."

"Yeah, I bloody well love her," Logan shot back. "Why do you think I left? I'm trying to do the right thing."

"How is walking away the right thing?"

"I can't give her an impressive last name or buy her a house like the one you two grew up in. I don't have a fancy degree, and the biggest inheritance in my future is Mr. Cuddles, my mum's mangy cat with a nasty personality."

"You know Kat doesn't give a shit about money."

"It's not just money. Don't you get it? I've got nothing to offer her, nothing she needs."

"You're kidding me, right? You don't see it?" Pax stared at Logan like he was a massive idiot, then shoved a hand through his hair and made a face. "Shit. You're going to make me say it, aren't you?"

"What the hell are you talking about?"

"Love, jackass," Pax snapped. "Love is what she needs, and you can give that to her. The way I look at it, you have two choices. You can walk away from the best thing that ever happened to you—leaving Kat heartbroken, alone, and thinking she wasn't enough to make you stay … " He walked to the door and paused.

Logan ground his teeth, his chest constricting in pain.

" … or you can stop being so fucking pathetic, tell her you love her, and beg her to give you a second chance. Worst case scenario, she says no and you're right back here—alone and depressing as fuck—but at least she'll know you loved her enough to try. And who knows?" Pax shrugged. "She might say yes, and you might not suck at being in it for the long haul. And one day you might even get your head out of your ass long enough to realize that you need her a hell of a lot more than she needs you."

Pax stomped out of the apartment and slammed the door behind him so hard the flimsy walls shook. "Dramatic bastard," Logan muttered, trying to ignore the hollow ache in his chest.

But Pax was right about one thing: Logan had

nothing more to lose. He'd left everything—his heart and his soul—behind with Kat. If there was a shot, no matter how slim, that she'd say yes to a future with him, then he had to take it. If nothing else, Kat deserved to know he loved her.

A shiver of unease snaked down his spine at the thought of how she'd react to seeing him again. Christ, she was going to eat him alive. Kat may be tiny, but she was fierce. And he'd not only been stupid enough to hurt her, he'd also been foolish enough to fall in love with her. He should have known better than to tangle with a tiger.

He never stood a chance of coming out of it unscathed.

FOURTEEN

WITH a grunt, Kat scooped up the last shovelful of snow and dumped it onto the large pile next to her. It was dusk on a cold December night, and the snow had finally stopped falling long enough for her to clear the sidewalk.

She had a sidewalk now. Actually she had a lot more than a sidewalk; she'd bought an updated two-story house in downtown Silver Bay a month ago. Shoveling snow wasn't the favorite task she'd acquired as a homeowner, but it had to be done.

"Need a hand?"

Kat straightened at the sound of the familiar male voice behind her. She jabbed the shovel into a pile of snow thick enough to hold it upright, slipped off a glove, and smoothed the stray dark hairs from her face as she turned around with a grin.

"Impressive timing. Did you wait until I was done before offering?"

"Nope." John grinned back at her. "I decided to stop by after I dug out Mrs. Dobolek's driveway.

Looks like I should have come here first."

"Don't be silly. Mrs. D. needs help shoveling. I don't. Besides, I think she likes you better than she likes me. Ever since you started helping her, she looks disappointed whenever I show up instead."

Kat grabbed the large container of environmentally friendly de-icer and started sprinkling it on the sidewalk. "Do you want to come inside for a cup of hot chocolate when I'm done?"

"Absolutely," John said, gently placing his hand on her shoulder and lifting the container away from her. "I'll finish up out here. You start on the drinks."

"Yeah, sure," Kat mumbled, tucking her chin down and turning away before he saw the tears in her eyes.

She still hadn't gotten used to the mass of unruly pregnancy hormones coursing through her system. In the past, a man trying to do something for her because she was a small female would have ticked her off. Now the simple gesture of helping her clean the sidewalk had her crying like an idiot.

She stepped into her foyer and stripped off her snow gear, thankful that under her coat she had on a super-sized black hoodie Logan had left behind in his haste to leave. Being about five sizes too big for her, the yards of extra fabric hid her expanding belly as much as possible. Of course, at this stage on her pregnancy, she wasn't going to be able to dodge curious questions from concerned citizens much longer.

She blew out a sigh and hooked her snow gear on the rack strategically hung over the floor heater. She'd put a lot of time and effort into making sure everything about her new place was perfect for her and her kiddo.

Her home sat on a pretty lot with some sort of big shady tree in the front and a secure looking fence enclosing the backyard. She'd bought the place from McKenna Wade, one of Claire's childhood girlfriends. Mac had been remodeling homes for a couple of years, and she'd spent over six months working on this one. Mac had opened up the floor plan, put down hardwood floors, and gutted the kitchen. From the inviting great room with a wood-burning fireplace to the modern kitchen with enough space to hold an oversized table, Kat loved everything about her new place.

She turned on the Christmas-tree lights and her favorite holiday music playlist as she crossed through the great room to the kitchen. By the time she had the mugs of chocolate ready and brimming with marshmallows, John stepped inside and hung his winter gear next to hers.

"Take a load off," Kat said, nodding toward her newly purchased couch as "White Christmas" started to play through her speakers in the living room.

John scanned the room as he sat down. "I can't believe all you've done in the past few months. Bought and furnished a house as well as taken over SAS full-time. How's that going, by the way?"

"SAS is great." She handed him a mug and sat in the leather chair perpendicular to the couch. "Both sets of seniors—the high schoolers and the elderly—seem to be enjoying each other's company. In fact, I'm not sure which is more entertained by the interaction. Two students stopped by Harry's house last week to help him set up a new printer, and somehow they got on the subject of fishing." Kat chuckled at the thought. "I don't know the details, but Harry told them about some sort of homemade lure that never fails. They're going back in the spring so he can show them how to make them."

"Probably the Jenkin twins. They're crazy about fishing." John took a sip of hot chocolate. "You're doing a good thing."

"Thanks." She grinned. "It's really fun bringing these two groups together. But there are some things the high schoolers just can't do. They're great at mowing lawns, raking leaves, and helping with electronics. But we can't ask them to drive to doctor's appointments or pick up medication—two requests we get a lot. So we're going to expand into the community to bring adults in to help as well."

"Count me in," John said. "Consider Mrs. Dobolek's driveway the first of many tasks."

"Has there ever been a cause, a kid, or a critter that you haven't volunteered to help?" she teased.

"Absolutely. I hate bees." He gave an exaggerated shiver. "I'll take off in a dead sprint if I hear or see one."

"And you admit that?"

"Can't exactly hide it when half the town has seen me running around blindly swatting the air around my head."

"I probably shouldn't tell you this, but Mac said she removed a nest of bees living under the deck."

"You still bought this place?" he asked with a tongue-in-cheek expression.

"Yep. I love it here. There are three bedrooms up and a full basement down."

"That's a lot of space for one person," he said with a meaningful look.

"I guess." She shrugged a shoulder and pretended to find the inside of her mug deeply interesting. She wasn't ashamed of her pregnancy— she just didn't want to talk about Logan. And any discussion about her baby would naturally lead to her baby's father.

"Kat," John said, waiting to continue until she met his eye. "Are you pregnant?"

She cocked an eyebrow. "I heard you weren't supposed to ask a woman that question unless you could actually see a baby coming out of her."

"Is that your way of telling me to butt out?"

"No," she sighed. "I'm happy to talk about my baby. Just not anyone else involved."

"He's not … coming back?"

Kat shook her head and sniffed. *Oh, hell.* Here come the waterworks. She wiped at the gathering tears and sniffed even louder. "Sorry. Hormones."

John swore under his breath, quickly kneeled in front of her, and took her hands in his. "I can't stand seeing you hurting like this. Let me take care of you. You don't have to be alone anymore."

"It's not your responsibility."

"Bullshit," he tightened his grip on her hands. "If someone I care about is hurting, and I can do something about it, then I damn well better do it."

"I know you, John. You want to save everyone and everything you meet. Remember those sickly kittens you insisted on finding homes for in junior high? They were scrawny and had some sort of nasty eye disease. Anyone else would have ignored them or turned them over to an animal shelter. Not you. Nope, you sweet talked Dr. Cambridge into treating them and then went door to door until you found families for each of them."

"I'd forgotten about that," he said, chuckling. "And I'm not even a cat person."

"Exactly! You didn't love them, but you still felt responsible for them. No way am I going to take advantage of you even if it would make my life easier."

"But I hate seeing you hurting like this," John said, his voice a rumble of sincerity.

"I know. That's one of the reasons you're such an amazing guy." Kat pulled her hand from his and traced her finger along his jaw. "But—and this is a big but—you don't love me," she said softly.

"Yes, I do," he argued, his face set in an adorably stubborn expression.

"Okay. Let me rephrase that. You love me like a friend, not a lover." She smothered a grin. "Want me to prove it to you?"

"Huh?"

Kat cupped his face in her hands and pulled him in for a big smooch on the lips, then sat back to take in his wide-eyed look. "See. No spark."

"Doesn't matter. Sparks don't last. They blind you with brightness for an instant, then they're gone." John tucked a strand of hair behind her ear the way Logan used to.

The tender gesture triggered unwanted memories and emotions. She knew time healed all wounds, but time needed to hurry the hell up. She hurt as much today as she did the day he left.

Kat drew in a big breath, expanding her chest in hopes of breaking sadness's tight grip around her heart. "You don't know how much I wish I'd fallen for you instead of him. But you deserve more than what you're willing to settle for."

"I want to help you."

She wrapped her arms around him and pulled him close. "You do help me. You're a great friend, and that's exactly what I need."

John sighed and hugged her back. "He's a fool."

"Yeah," she agreed with a sad laugh. "But for some screwed-up reason, I still love him."

Three loud knocks drew Kat's attention to her front door. "I'd better get that," she said, glancing at the clock on her mantle.

Everyone in her very concerned family had been treating her like she was as fragile as an egg shell since she'd told them about the pregnancy. Whichever one of them was checking up on her tonight must be in a rush. Her door had actually rattled from the pounding.

The demanding knock sounded again before she reached the foyer. "Chill," she muttered swinging the door open.

Her heart lurched at the sight of the man frozen in place on her doorstep. He was staring at her with a mixed look of trepidation and determination in his crystal-blue eyes.

"Logan, what the hell are you wearing?" She regretted the words the minute they left her mouth. Questioning his wardrobe hadn't once been on the list of colorful things she'd daydreamed about saying to him since he'd left her.

He blinked in surprise, glanced down at himself, and then back up at her. "Uh, clothes," he answered with a confused expression.

She rolled her eyes and crossed her arms over her chest. "Well, duh. I meant, why aren't you wearing a winter coat? Or a hat, boots, or gloves? It's freezing out, and you're dressed for a sunny fall day." She threw her hands up in the air. "You know what? Never mind. You left. I don't give a shit what you wear. You can freeze your stupid ass off for all I care." Kat grabbed the door and swung it at him. Hard.

Logan shot his arm out to stop the door from slamming into his face. "We need to talk," he said, stepping inside. "Alone," he growled at John standing behind her.

John placed a hand on her shoulder. "Do you want me to get rid of him?"

Logan's eyes blazed. "Sorry, mate, no one's getting rid of me."

"Oh, now you want to stay?" Kat poked Logan in the chest. "Last time, you couldn't leave fast enough. What changed your mind, big guy?"

Logan stepped closer, looking completely miserable. "Kat, I never—"

In a flash of movement, John's fist hit Logan's jaw with a sickening thud. Logan's head snapped to the side. For a split second, he froze like that, then he turned back and took a step toward John, eyes blazing again.

"Stop!" Kat jumped between the two men and put one hand on each of their chests. "The last thing I need is blood splatters on my freshly painted walls."

"He deserved it," John mumbled, rubbing his hand.

"Kat, we need to talk, and we can't do that with your *boyfriend* here."

"The lady has nothing to say to you." John's

chest pushed harder into her hand as he leaned toward Logan with a sneer.

"That's none of your damn business." Logan shot back, stepping toward John.

Kat rolled her eyes again, gave both of their chests an irritated shove, and turned toward John. "I do need to talk to him. It's okay," she said with a reassuring smile. "I'll be fine."

John stared at her for a long, tense moment. Then he huffed out a resigned sigh. "Call if you need me." He dropped a kiss on top of her head, gathered his snow gear, and checked his shoulder into Logan's as he strode out of the house.

Pretending to ignore Logan, Kat shut the door and walked to the kitchen. She could feel him follow her. *Ugh*. Her body still hummed when he was near. She tore off a couple of paper towels and shoved them at him. "Stop bleeding all over my house."

Logan grinned and pushed the wad of paper against the blood on his lip. "I've missed your warm, affectionate nature, tiger."

She flipped him off and leaned back against the smooth quartz countertop.

"I deserved that."

She didn't argue.

He scanned his gaze down her body and quirked an eyebrow. "Nice hoodie."

"Yeah. You left a lot of great stuff behind." She cocked her head and studied him with feigned indifference. "Why are you here?"

He tensed and drew in two quick breaths as if preparing for battle. "I want you to give me a second chance."

She stared at him. "I thought you didn't stick.

With anyone."

"I want to. With you," he said, his body humming with intensity.

The fact that he didn't mention loving her didn't go unnoticed. "So why'd you leave?" Her voice cracked with strain, totally negating the cool vibe she was trying so hard to project.

"Thought I couldn't make you happy long-term." He turned away to pace her kitchen. "Couldn't go through that again, so I took off before you came to your bloody senses and told me to get lost."

"Again?"

Logan stopped pacing and looked at her. "What?"

"You said 'again.' What did you mean?"

He snapped his mouth shut and stared at her mutely. She crossed her arms and glared right back. He'd come to her house wanting to talk, so let him talk.

He inhaled slowly, blew it out, and rubbed the back of his neck with a distant expression on his face. "I told you about the country club I worked at in Sydney. Well, I dated a rich girl that I met there whose family made more in one week than my mum did in a year." Logan gave a mirthless laugh. "I didn't think it mattered to her or her family that I didn't come from money. Her parents seemed to like me. They even invited me to their fancy parties and introduced me to their rich friends."

"Did you love her?"

"Thought I did. When I was eighteen, I sold my motorbike to pay for a ring. Planned this whole romantic day for her that ended up with me on one knee." He paused and scrubbed a hand down his face as if as if trying to wipe away the memory.

"She said no," Kat finished softly, trying to save Logan from having to say it.

"She thought I was kidding." His voice and his features were flat, distant, resigned. But he couldn't hide the deep-rooted pain she saw in his beautiful blue eyes. "She stopped laughing and started apologizing when she realized I was serious. Said she just wanted a little fun before going to university. Said her parents would disown her if she married a guy like me—a guy meant for fun not for the future."

Logan clenched his fists at his sides and locked his eyes on her, waiting for a response.

Kat tipped her chin up and stared right back at him. Anger filling her chest and hardening her features. "Good," she snapped.

He jerked back, obviously not expecting that response.

"If you're looking for sympathy, you came to the wrong person. I'm happy she turned you down. Otherwise … " She took a step forward and poked him in the chest. "You'd be married to her and living in Australia. And I would've never met you."

His eyes softened at her words. "Tiger, I—"

"I'm not done, big guy." She drew in a breath and placed her palm over his heart. "I am sorry she hurt you, but I'm frickin' thrilled she was too damn stupid to realize your kindness, humor, intelligence, and strength made you the perfect guy to have around then, now … forever."

His jaw clenched with emotion. "I can't believe you're defending me."

"I guess it kinda helps to understand why you won't commit."

"After her, I made damn sure my relationships stayed simple." Intensity edged his voice. "Then you crashed into my life and nothing's been simple since."

"You have no idea," she barely said it. He heard her anyway.

"What do you mean?" he asked.

Before she lost her nerve, Kat stepped back, grabbed the hem of the oversized hoodie, pulled it over her head, and tossed it onto the countertop. She smoothed her hands over the unmistakable baby bump under her stretchy white shirt and took in Logan's wide-eyed expression.

"I'm pregnant." She closed her eyes for a beat and fought to control the anxiety rattling around inside of her. "Don't worry. I have no unrealistic expectations on how this is going to play out. You can be involved as little or as much as you want."

Logan's shocked gaze darted from her expanding belly to her face to her belly again. He took a jerky step forward and stopped, clearly unsure what to do next. "How?" he eventually stammered, a wide range of emotions playing across his face.

She quirked an eyebrow in response.

"Fine. I know *how* it happened." He scrubbed a hand down his face again and leaned his butt against the kitchen island, looking like he might topple over without the support. "I just don't know *how* it happened."

"Not sure." She shrugged one shoulder. "Maybe faulty protection, user error, vigorous swimmers able to bust through normal barriers, or ... " She spanned her belly with both hands. "Fate."

"Fate?" Logan froze for a beat, then his face split into a wide smile. "I like the sound of that."

She blew out a massive breath as relief flooded through her. "You don't know how good that is to hear."

"After I decided to never attempt another serious relationship, I reckoned I'd never be a dad. Guess fate reckoned otherwise."

Before she could respond, a thunk in her belly knocked the air from her lungs. "Holy hell!" Kat gripped her swollen belly harder. "Oh! I mean holy heck."

"What's wrong?" Logan shot forward, instantly alert.

She felt another jab and smiled like an idiot. "He kicked me. The baby kicked me. Not surprising considering I'm shaking with adrenaline right now." She grabbed Logan's hands and placed them flat to her belly and held her breath. Sure enough, their little guy kicked again.

Dropping to his knees, he held her rounded belly in both hands. "He?" Logan looked up to meet her gaze, elation and amazement lighting his face.

She chewed her lip and smiled down at Logan. "You have a son."

He grinned back then turned his full attention to her belly. "Hey, mate, that's an ace kick you've got there," he murmured. "I'm your dad and ... " He broke off as his words shook and his face contorted with emotion. He drew in a long breath and exhaled slowly. "And I can be a bloody idiot at times, but I'll do my best to do right by you. I promise that I'll always be there for you." He leaned forward and kissed her belly. "And I'll always love you."

Fighting tears, Kat sniffed and smoothed Logan's hair with her hands as he kissed her belly again. Her chest swelled with joy, sadness, relief, regret, and a hundred other conflicting, confusing emotions. No matter how happy his declaration of eternal love to their child made her, Kat ached for him to make a similar promise to her.

With a mental eye roll, she cursed her stupidity. Logan had told her from the beginning that he didn't do love, and she'd arrogantly ignored the warning and fallen for him anyway. While hearing about his past explained why he would never trust a woman with his heart again, it only explained, not changed the depressing fact. He'd asked for a second chance, but he'd never mentioned love.

Weariness seeped into her soul. Over the last year, she'd gotten good at burying her emotions. Employing the trick again, she forced a grin. "No worries, mate. You're going to be a great dad," she said, imitating his accent.

Logan gave her a grateful smile as he rose to stand in front of her again. "Thanks for the encouragement." He dropped his head and kneaded the back of his neck with one hand. "I've never been so bloody happy, proud, and scared in my life."

Kat sighed as forgiveness and empathy continued to work their way into the cracks of her broken heart. "I thought nothing could scare you."

Head still dipped, Logan chuckled. "Are you kidding? I fell in love with a tiger. Do you have any idea how terrifying that is?"

Her mouth dropped open, and her heart stilled. A second later, it thudded back to life, pounding wildly in her chest. "You love me?"

He looked up, his mouth curved in a sad smile. "Of course, I love you, Kat. I love that fiery spirit, quick wit, and sharp tongue. I love that you're challenging, cheeky, and charming all at the same time. I love that you'd rather help people than be helped. And most of all, I love that big, soft heart you try so hard to hide."

"I ... I didn't know." She stumbled over the words, unable to believe she just might get her frickin' happily-ever-after after all.

"Ah, tiger, I love you as much as I love that baby in your belly. But, unlike him, you're not stuck with me." Logan stepped closer to tuck a strand of hair behind her ear. He let his hand linger alongside her face for a moment, then he dropped it away. "All I can do now is tell you how sorry I am for hurting you and ask for a second chance. Please let me love you, Kat. If you say yes, I promise to do every damn thing in my power to make you happy for the rest of your life."

"Logan, I—"

"Wait," he interrupted, looking determined and utterly adorable. "Before you answer, you should know that wanker will never understand you, appreciate the spark in your eyes, or love you a fraction as much as I do."

"Wanker?"

"That idiot boyfriend of yours." Logan nodded toward the door. "John."

"John and I aren't together." She bit back a grin.

"I saw you kiss him through the window," he said, brows drawn in confusion.

"That wasn't a real kiss." She waved away his

words. "I was proving a point. John and I don't spark."

He stepped closer, intensity radiating from every inch of him. "We spark," he said in a low, husky voice.

"Big guy, we more than spark." Kat put her hand on his chest, feeling heat instantly burn through her. "We blaze."

He laid a hand over hers. "Have I lost you, Kat? Or can you forgive me for walking away?"

She blew out a breath and shook her head. "I've already forgiven you. Love makes it too damn hard to hold a grudge."

Logan's eyes widened and his grip tightened on her hand. "You love me?" Emotion rumbled through his deep voice.

"Yeah. I love you, Logan McCabe. And I'm sorry for hurting you too. I was wrong before," she continued, stepping closer and tilting her head back to hold his gaze. "I do need you. I need you in my life and by my side, loving me as much as I love you." She sucked in a breath and made a face. "How much is all this freaking you out?"

"Actually, being in this together makes the whole thing a lot less scary," he said with a boyish smile. He lifted his gaze to look around her home, contemplating. "Your place is big enough. Maybe I could crash with you for a while."

"Hmm." Kat cocked an eyebrow. "How long were you thinking?"

"How's forever sound?"

Biting back a smile, Kat stretched to her tiptoes, slipped her arms around Logan's neck, and pulled him closer. "With you, big guy," she murmured, her lips an instant from his, "forever sounds ace."

EPILOGUE

KAT kicked off her heeled sandals and wiggled her toes on the cool, rough brick beneath the elaborately set table on the southern edge of her parents' sprawling outdoor patio. The welcome breeze blowing in from the lake cooled the warm summer evening to perfection. And with Logan beside her and their three-month-old son, Bennett, sleeping snugly against her chest, Kat knew a thing or two about perfection.

They were seated with her family—including the recently engaged Sage and Pax who'd flown in from Costa Rica—at a hand-carved, solid-wood outdoor table custom made by Bennett Industry's finest craftsmen. Richard had given the table to his wife that morning as a present for her sixtieth birthday. It could seat ten comfortably, twelve if the diners liked coziness.

Tonight was the culmination of a multi-day celebration of their mom's milestone birthday, hence the need for the large table. Of course, at the recent rate of family expansion, her mom might need a new table soon. Kat smiled at the thought, dropped a kiss onto her son's sweet-smelling little head, and then slid one hand to rest on Logan's muscled thigh.

Logan lifted her hand in his for a soft kiss. "When are you going to tell them?" he murmured against her skin with a pleased, proud, sexy-as-sin look in his eye.

"Don't rush me," Kat whispered with a wink. "I've planned a little speech that's lovely and really sentimental. I wanna say it at just the right time."

He raised a skeptical eyebrow.

"What? I can do sentimental. I'm totally going to nail this."

"Thank you for that wonderful dinner." Her mom's smiling voice pulled their attention to the head of the table. "Sharing a meal with my children and grandchildren was the absolute perfect way to spend my birthday."

"The celebration isn't over yet," Hannah said, standing up. "I just need to add a few finishing touches to your cake before it's ready. Ty and Grace, do you want to help?"

With enthusiastic agreement, Kat's niece and nephew hopped up from their seats—likely happy for the chance to score some frosting from Hannah before dessert was even served.

"I'll come too." Sage pushed her chair back. "I'm going to take that handsome guy with me. I've been staring across the table at him all night and can't wait any longer to get my hands on him."

"You better be talking about the kid," Pax grumbled.

After shooting Pax a saucy smile, Sage walked

around the table, carefully scooped up Bennett, and cradled him in her arms with a wistful expression. The little guy stirred for a moment then relaxed back into sleep.

"I want one." She sighed plenty loud for Pax to hear as she walked toward the patio door.

"Looks like you're next, mate."

"I'm focusing on the wedding first." Pax gave Logan an easy smile. "There are a few things we need to take care of at La Vida before the ceremony there in December. Like finding a new adventure guide and surf instructor."

"Sorry about that, but I'm needed here." Logan brushed another warm kiss along Kat's knuckles and eyed her with that sexy, half-lidded look of his that instantly made her best parts take notice.

"I can see that." Pax cleared his throat. "Now stop eyeballing my little sister and tell me about your new personal-training facility. I hear it's a hit."

"My schedule is full nearly every day of the week. Seems people are happy to have a place in Silver Bay to work out. They also like that I personalize regimens based on individual fitness goals."

"It's the talk of the town," Richard interjected proudly. "I train with him three times a week. I haven't been in such good shape since I was your age."

"I go in every Thursday morning for a small group session with book-club friends," Ann added.

"A mighty rowdy bunch they are. Your mum's the only one who behaves."

"Well, yes, a few ladies are a bit overzealous," Ann said, looking away and smoothing her already perfectly smooth hair.

"Overzealous?" Kat scoffed. "Logan had to enforce a 'hands off' policy for your friends specifically."

Pax cringed. "Sorry I asked."

"What can I say? The ladies love me." Logan shot him a cheeky grin.

Kat rolled her eyes and elbowed Logan in the side. "We've gotta do something about that ego of yours."

"How's SAS?" Pax asked Kat in a not-so-subtle attempt to change the subject.

"Great. I'm working on our first major fundraiser. It's going to be a big fall festival in the town square. Ever since Claire agreed to help, I've been securing a ton of great volunteers for the event."

Claire wrinkled her nose. "That's odd. People are usually quick to volunteer for a good cause. Why does it matter if I'm doing it or not."

Kat shrugged. "Probably because it's the first year of a new event."

Logan chuckled beside her. "Yeah, tiger, let's run with that theory."

Claire's sharp gaze focused on Logan. "Why are you laughing?"

She shot her attention to Kat. "Why is he laughing?"

"No reason." Kat gave Claire a serene smile and elbowed Logan again, only harder this time. "Ignore him. He's easily amused."

"That's true," Logan acknowledged with a devilish grin. "But you're still going to have to tell her sometime."

"Yes, dear," Ann said to Kat. "Claire will need a

little time to process her role in the fundraiser."

Claire's eyes widened, then instantly narrowed to focus on each person in turn. "Does everyone know about this except me?"

Pax shot his hands up in a don't-look-at-me gesture.

"Somebody better start talking. Now."

"Chill out, Claire. It's totally no biggie." Kat grinned, shooing away her sister's concern with a few flicks of her wrist. "For the showcase event we're auctioning off dates with some of the town's most eligible bachelors and bachelorettes."

Claire's expression went from anxious to dumbstruck in about two point two seconds. "And I'm one of the eligible bachelorettes?" she squeaked.

"Damn. Good thing Cosmo's not here." Kat peered around the yard dramatically. "You could've blown out the poor dog's hearing with that last note."

"No way," Claire stated, determination etched on her face.

"I'm serious. Dogs have very sensitive hearing."

"I meant," Claire gritted out, "no way am I standing on a stage to be auctioned off to the highest bidder. Is that even legal?"

"It's just one date. Besides it will be good for you. Shake up your routine a little."

"Huh uh. Nope. Not happening." Claire couldn't seem to stop shaking her head.

"You're a bigwig at Bennett Industries and well respected in town. Every other bachelor and bachelorette agreed to participate once I told them you were doing it. If you back out now, the whole fundraiser could fall apart."

"I'm sorry to say that Kat's right," Richard said, patting Claire's hand. "As much as it pains me to think of men bidding on a date with one of my daughters, this is an important event for SAS."

Claire's face fell. "I hate being the center of attention. I can't stand on a stage like an idiot praying that someone, anyone bids on me." She turned her pleading gaze to her sister. "You should do it, Kat. You'd bring in a ton of money."

"Not gonna happen," Logan stated firmly.

Claire glared at Logan a moment, then relented. "Fine," she snapped, turning back to her sister. "There has to be some way out of this."

"I'll tell you the same thing I told everyone else. If you become involved in a serious relationship between now and the auction, you can gracefully bow out."

Claire perked up in interest.

"And I'm not talking about a date or two, sister of mine. I'm talking about a committed relationship that you've acknowledged in public."

Before Claire could respond, the back door flew open, and Ty and Grace came running out, followed by Hannah carrying an elegant two-tier ivory cake that looked big enough to feed fifty. It had a slightly larger bottom tier with an intricate pearl beading design of pale lavender frosting wrapped around the base. The smaller top tier, however, held the real focal point of the cake—an artistic scattering of large, life-like roses and lilacs in multiple coordinating shades of lavender and pale-pink frosting.

While everyone else oohed and aahed over the culinary masterpiece, Claire turned to Kat. "I can't do it," she hissed. "Don't you remember what happened the last time I was on stage in my fourth-grade production of *A Christmas Carol*? I got so nervous that I threw up all over Tiny Tim. The kids called me the Ghost of Christmas Puke for the rest of the year!"

"Oh, yeah," Kat grinned at the memory. "Guess it's time to face your fears."

Claire glared at her in the pale moonlight, then after a beat, nodded toward the head of the table. "Mom's about to blow out the candles. We'll discuss the fundraiser later."

Kat huffed out a sigh. Her big sister needed to stop overthinking everything and embrace spontaneity for once in her life.

Kat waited until cake had been served and enjoyed, then stretched up to kiss Logan on the cheek. "Ready to head home, big guy?" she whispered in his ear.

Instant heat darkened his eyes to midnight. "Good-oh. I'll try to wrestle Bennett away from your mum. It might take awhile."

Kat watched Logan amble toward her mom. After chatting for a minute, he gently extricated their recently awakened son from his doting grandmother's arms and gave him a big kiss on his pudgy little cheek.

Kat's chest swelled with love. "We're heading out." She slipped on her sandals, rose from the table, and walked to stand next to Logan and Bennett. "Everyone can still make it to the cookout at our place Saturday night, right?"

The family all gave her some sort of confirmation.

"Topnotch." She wrapped an arm around Logan's waist. "Appetizers are at six. The ceremony is at seven. We'll grill out afterward. See you then." She nudged Logan to leave, but his big body didn't budge.

Sage gasped. "Ceremony?"

"You're getting married in three days?" Pax asked, looking a bit shell-shocked.

"Yip." Pride rang through Logan's deep voice as he held Bennett tightly in one arm and wrapped his other around Kat's shoulders.

"Oh, how wonderful." Ann clasped her hands in excitement.

" 'Bout time," her dad grumbled, reaching for another piece of cake.

"You're right, Dad." Kat snuggled against Logan's side and playful patted his chest. "It is time I made an honest man out of him."

After a moment of shocked silence, an explosion of questions and excited chatter erupted as everyone started talking at once. Startled at the commotion, Bennett bunched his adorable face in concern. If they didn't get the little guy away from here soon, he was going to give his vocal cords one heck of a workout.

"That's our cue," she said to Logan, grabbing his arm and steering him toward the stone path at the edge of the patio. "Sorry," she tossed to her family over one shoulder. "Gotta go. It's Bennett's bedtime."

Logan cocked an eyebrow as she hustled him around the corner of the house. "You and I have very different definitions of sentimental, darl."

"Sorry. Guess I'm not the sentimental type after

all." She clicked her tongue and winked. "Too bad you're a man of your word. You're stuck with me now."

Logan grinned down at her, his blue eyes dancing with amusement, patience, and love. "I don't feel stuck, tiger. But with you and with him,"—he nodded toward their son—"I'll damn sure always stick."

Thank You!

Thanks for reading Crashing Together*! I hope you enjoyed it, and I hope you'll consider taking a moment to write a quick review. Even one or two sentences about a book can help readers and authors alike.*

Book three in the Silver Bay series, Lucky in Love*, features Claire Bennett's romance and will be available near the end of 2017. If you'd like to receive an email on release day, please visit www.ameliajudd.com to join my VIP list.*

Happy reading!
Amelia

About the Author

Award-winning author Amelia Judd writes fun and flirty contemporary romance. She loves to entertain her readers with memorable characters and fast-paced plots that blend humor, heart, and heat.

After receiving a degree in international affairs, Amelia lived and studied in Belgium for over three years. During her time in Europe, she traveled extensively, earned a master's degree, and fell in love with writing contemporary romance.

Amelia now lives in the Midwest with her sports-loving husband, two active kids, and a lovable dog that insists on staying by her side day and night. When she isn't writing, she's spending time with family, hanging out with friends, chauffeuring her kiddos around town, sneaking off to the movies, or planning her family's next getaway.

Connect with Amelia online:

www.ameliajudd.com

www.facebook.com/author.amelia.judd/

amelia@ameliajudd.com

www.goodreads.com/Amelia_Judd